HERBIE VOAR:
The Memoirs

as told to
Frank Renwick
the Baron of Ravenstone

978-0-9513913-4-1

RAVENSTONE PRESS 2011
Printed and produced by McKenzie Quality Print, Aberdeen

CONTENTS

1. Early Days .... Page 1
2. School Days 6
3. I Join the Pansies 13
4. With Jock Force in the Jungle 19
5. Sergeant Voar on Parade 25
6. On Leave 28
7. Boomtime in Upswapo 31
8. Blessed Assurance Branches Out 34
9. Away up North 37
10. Aunty Vyra Goes to Church 43
11. Ertie Moves wi' da Times 49
12. Saga of Susie Wong 52
13. Bonzo Dog's Big Offer 60
14. Magongograd 63
15. Bye Bye Comrades 68
16. Invasion 70
17. The Upswapo War 74
18. Stubs and Burt Bite the Dust 77
19. A Sailor's Farewell 80
20. Governor of Gwelo 84
21. Bugs 'n Rugs 90
22. Jumbo Trotter Spills the Beans 94
23. Ngwozo 99
24. Madame Mafudi Extends a Welcome 102
25. Ramon Hitches a Lift 106
26. Ambush 111
27. Basket Case 115
28. Kibugoma 118
29. Trixie Pulls it Off 121
30. Ludo 124
31. A Wrastle wi' Mistah Blotts 131
32. Come Day, Go Day 137
33. The Great White Queen 140
34. Herbie's New Hobby 145
35. In the Valley of the Pharaohs 149

BOOKS BY THE SAME AUTHOR

NOOST (1978)

SCOTLAND BLOODY SCOTLAND (1986 et seq)

THE TUPPER REPORT (1988)

EUROPE BLOODY EUROPE (1992)

GRABOLA (1994)

GOOFLA (1999)

LEEBSTER MACKAY, THE KICKIEDOURIE DICK (2002)

THE COMPLEAT LODE OF CARP (2006)

CHAPTER 1: EARLY DAYS.

One of my earliest memories is of lying in bed, along with my eight brothers and sisters, listening to the bugle sounding reveille at the Fort. That was during the War of course. Bertie the Bugler we used to call him, though his real name was Bertie Flaws, from Rousay in Orkney, who later married Mother's sister Marabelle. They had a pub in Stromness after the War, and later did all right I believe, before the drink took its toll. But of course, then he was in the Royal Corps of Buglers.

PETER WONOOK FAMILY BUTCHER — wir hom ↑

At that time we were living in the old North Road, in a shed up behind Uncle Peter's butcher shop. It was a bit cramped by modern standards maybe, but what we lacked in refinements we made up for in togetherness. There was a bogey stove that burned peats and kept us all warm about the nights, and a toilet at the bottom of the lane, made from three tea chests. People had to use whatever came to hand in those days, of course, in our case bits of People's Friend that Mother used to string together and hang on a nail in there, fine reading as well as useful. You don't get anything like literary toilet paper nowadays.

Our Dad, Robbie Voar – Big Robbie as he was always called if you didn't want trouble – was a Foula man, a place well known for big men, and Mother was from Mid Yell a place well known for big women. It wasn't easy for them fitting into the shed, especially after they had nine – later eleven (or was it thirteen ?) – children, but we all managed somehow, and, of course on looking back, they were halcyon days. Mother was a Wonook from Mid Yell, her father being Herbert Wonook, skipper of the Laughing Trow, after whom yours truly was named – Herbert I mean, not the Trow – my full name being Herbert MacFadzeon Voar. It was the custom, thenadays to give the Church of Scotland Minister's surname to a boy as a middle name, Rev. Thomas MacFadzeon being the minister in the big manse there at the time. There were quite a few Yell boys named after him, though the rumour that Rev. MacFadzeon had a bit more to do with their begetting than mere baptism was generally dismissed as idle tittle-tattle. Of course, in those days, a Church of Scotland minister was not someone you would dare to question. He later became minister of the Auld Kirk in Lerwick.

The Voars of course, are a well known Foula family, and have been for many generations. Big men are no rarity among them, and they can turn their hands and brains to just about everything, except maybe getting out of bed. At this time our Dad, big Robbie, having come to the Mainland of Shetland to find employment as a dock worker with Messrs Mansons, was a prisoner of war of the Germans, having been captured at Dunkirk and interned in a Stalag for the duration of hostilities, leaving our Mother to raise the fourteen of us as best she could. Times were hard, but no one thought anything of it and we just got on with it.

Discipline was strict in those days. Mother kept a stout, brass-buckled leather belt that had belonged to Auld Jeemsie Voar hanging on a nail near the bogey stove, and it certainly wasn't there for decoration. Many's

Big Rothie

the time she would lay about her and, of course, cooped up as we were like hens in a henhouse, it was not easy to dodge her blows, especially if she'd keyed the door first and extracted the key. It never did us any harm of course, and we soon grew accustomed to her outbursts. And then, as she also worked long hours gutting and packing herring for Messrs Hoseason, there were many summer days when she was hardly ever there. To prepare for such absences she would boil up a large cauldron of porridge and pour it into a drawer in the dresser. Then Rosie, my eldest sister, had the daily job of cutting a slice for each of us every morning, which kept us going through the day. A drawerful would last a week, though by week's end the slices were usually getting pretty thin. And a bit mouldy. If we were really lucky, Rosie would come up with a bit of dripping and we'd fry our slices in the frying pan on the stove. Yummy! At least keeping it in the drawer kept the rats off it, though once – only once, it never happened again – Rosie left the drawer open and the rats had a picnic.

Myself when young.

Sundays being then regarded as the Lord's Day, saw us all packed off to Sunday School, and Mother got an all-too-brief period of rest and relaxation, a time she usually spent with a

3

bottle of stout and her feet up, reading the previous week's News of the World. Our Sunday School teacher, Nettie MacPhail from Bixter, was one of the old school. She dinned in the Shorter Catechism by reminding us frequently of the torments of Hell that awaited all slackers. It was her speciality to make us learn all the books of the Bible by heart, then say them in reverse order without hesitation. This was supposed to keep all those who managed this theological feat safe from the Evil One. You were also awarded a pandrop. It may seem a bit draconian nowadays, but many's the man who in later life came to bless Nettie's efforts when he found himself confronted with perils and temptations, and dealt with them by repeating the books of the Bible backwards.

Miss MacPhail - Sunday School Teacher

The highlight of our Sunday School year was the annual Picnic, and the highlight of the picnic was the bag of buns each of us received, the only buns I or my siblings saw throughout the year. Of course, if you hadn't attended regularly you got no buns, and if you couldn't say the Books in reverse order you only got half a bag. All of this stood us in good stead later on.

Our Dad returned home in 1946 with many tales to tell of life in the Stalag. It had not been all bad, however, for he had chummed up with a fellow Shetlander, Ertie Spence from Bixter, and one of the officers, Captain Spalding, who had been an insurance man in civvy street. Together, they explored the various possibilities of insurance, or "the protection racket" as Captain Spalding called it, and before they were all repatriated at the end of the War, Captain Spalding issued both of them with impressive certificates which he'd spent considerable time manufacturing in the Stalag recreation block, qualifying them as bona fide Insurance Men and holders of the official Degree of the Institute of Insurance Practitioners. Dad was very proud of his impressive looking document and later made a fancy mahogany frame for it to hang on the wall. Ertie rented an attic room above Cossar's Gentlemens Outfitters, in Commercial Street, where

Ertie Spence

Capt. Spalding.

they set up Blessed Assurance, Ltd. and commenced banging on the doors of the new Council estates to persuade the inhabitants that they needed Insurance like a drowning man needs a lifebelt. It was certainly different from dock labouring.

Next year, we were ourselves allotted a Council House, No. 8 Provost Freebie Drive, Lerwick. Certainly by that time, with the fifteen of us in Uncle Peter's shed, and some of us a good bit bigger, as well as Dad now having to do a bit of paper work when he came home about the nights, we were fairly short of space. Our new home was thus a considerable improvement with three bedrooms, a kitchen with a gas cooker, sitting room and a bathroom and toilet indoors. To say we were all delighted is no exaggeration, though finding the rent probably took most of Dad's wages. He must have had a little left over though, for it wasn't long after we moved in that he bought a second-hand bicycle and used it thereafter on his rounds. Things were looking up for the Voars!

No. 8, Provost Freebie Drive.

5

CHAPTER 2 : SCHOOL DAYS.

Life for us children was certainly full of interest and opportunity in those days, and the familiar words "Mam I'm bored" were never heard. The other boys on the Estate looked at first upon us newcomers askance and called us "Hutties," a term that included any who had been rehoused from their previous dwellings in wooden huts, tin sheds, fish boxes, holes in the ground and other fine old basic Shetland residences. It soon became evident to us, however, – there being nine of us Voar boys plus an assortment of other "Hutties" – that we could marmalize the rest without much effort. This we proceeded to do, and soon all the children on the Estate were under our protection, all children not in our gang being required to pay a weekly freewill offering – as it is known in Church circles – from their pocket money if they wanted out to play in peace without being duffed up. Even wee girls paid us. Soon, benefitting from our Biblical knowledge, we changed our gang name to "Huttites" (Ebeneezers 15: 11: "And the Lord blessed the Huttites and led them into a land flowing with milk and honey") the whole estate eventually becoming known as Huttieland, with its very own anthem set to the tune of a well-known hymn :

> There is a Huttieland far far away,
> Where all the children stand, lined up to pay.
> "Pay up!" their voices cry, "If you don't you're going to die,
> "You'll be away up in the sky, Far, far away"

As an insurance man, Dad was quick to commend our youthful initiative. Like many another father returning home after the War he had stuffed a few Nazi keepsakes in his kitbag which he now distributed among us by way of presents: SS daggers, hand grenades, tank shells, bayonets, etc. Among children they were just curious playthings but some of us were no longer children: we'd put on weight and shot up, a tribute to the health giving properties of cold sliced porridge. When the dark nights set in, we were out and about terrorising adults as well as children, lobbing the occasional grenade through a front door, or skewering the occasional moggie to a front lawn. As Dad explained when he called on the anxious householders, "What else could you expect in the aftermath of six years of war?" We were living in dangerous times, he said. Fortunately, he was glad to be able to tell them that Blessed Assurance had just the right policy to cover such eventualities. Folk soon found that in return for 2/6 a week paid promptly to Big Robbie or one of his little helpers, they were left in peace. It wasn't long before Dad was able to trade in his bike and get a second hand Morris car – the first ever motor in Provost Freebie Drive. The days when the Huttites were poor relations were definitely gone.

It was about this time that I must have started in the Secondary department of the old Commercial School. I cannot remember much about the Primary School except that we had to learn ten spellings every night and were belted every morning if we scored less than seven out of ten, which was fair enough, for being able to spell is a definite advantage in the big wide world. Quite a few children used to rub bits of soap on their palms in preparation for this ritual, but we despised them as softies and anyway, soap was a rarity in our house. The belt was in daily use. It also helped us learn our multiplication tables, lots of historic dates, capitals of countries, rivers of various continents and considerable mathematical feats such as Money Long Division which, with the old Pounds, Shillings and Pence was certainly no doddle. I shouldn't think today's youngsters would enjoy that overmuch.

Teachers were like Ministers in those days: the ordinary mortal would never question them. If you were belted at school for bad behaviour or slackness and your Mum or Dad got to hear about it, you'd probably get worse from them. In the Primary, I'd say it was definitely an aid to learning, but often with some Secondary teachers, it was too often used because the teachers were useless or in a bad mood. Also, as you changed teachers every forty minutes or so and there were seven such periods in a school day, you could, at least in theory, be belted by seven different stalwarts between nine o'clock in the morning and four in the afternoon. Some lads claimed to have had this educative experience several times. Not that it mattered that much. In Shetland, I would say, you learned at least as much outside school as inside and, in our case at least, our Dad usually took an interest in our activities.

I already had two brothers – Herkie and Bazz – at the Secondary and three sisters. We decided to start up a branch of the Huttites there, recruiting a few other pals from Huttieland to help us put the screw on the other pupils. Naturally, we met with a fair bit of initial resistance, leading directly to fighting which mushroomed in due course into what could, with little exaggeration, be described as open warfare and widespread mayhem. Despite their best efforts and worst threats, the Head Man and his staff failed to discover what the disturbance was about – anyone who grassed was disposed of over the Knab with a concrete block tied to his or her foot – and they had to restrict themselves to wiping up the mess, caring for the disabled and making generalisations about the War. Occasionally one of our members was caught with an SS dagger or a bayonet down his trousers. Once, the Geography department was demolished when a hand grenade went off accidentally. But all in all, it was a war that played itself out against a backdrop of scholastic endeavour. The individual peculiarities and belting habits of staff paled by comparison.

Aald Leebie

There were, however, some memorable teachers at the old Comm. Aald Leebie was one such. The Navigation teacher had served her youth in some of the last sailing brigs in the Great Southern Ocean. No one knew how old she was and no one dared to ask. If there was one teacher who had no need of a belt, it was Aald Leebie, for she was known to have felled a stirk in Whalsay where she came from, with one chop of her meaty fist. In appearance she resembled a herring barrel with two stout legs, two thick arms and a square head stuck on top. She walked – or rolled rather – accordingly. Every lunchtime she rolled down to Magnie's Speakeasy at the harbour and sat in there till ten minutes to two, eating pies and drinking stout, before rolling back uphill again to get into school at two o'clock precisely, despite the fact that afternoon classes started at one thirty. No one thought it their business to tell her that. Generations of Shetland seamen swore by the grounding Aald Leebie gave them, and certificates signed by her were as good as college diplomas anywhere on earth.

Leebie's funeral in the Aald Kirk was one of the biggest I've ever seen. It was attended by mariners from all over the world. Following the service, conducted by Rev. MacFadzeon, her coffin was placed aboard an old hulk, the Valhalla Princess, towed out into the middle of Bressay Sound and set ablaze, raising Leebie to the City of Gold on massive flames, while the men on the boats all around sang Will Your Anchor Hold. They don't make funerals like that nowadays.

The Headmaster when I went there first was old Dodo Halcrow, who'd been there since the early Thirties at least, and was probably losing his grip for he certainly failed to get a grip on the Huttites, who had the place pretty well sewn up by 1949, when Dodo's successor was appointed. Dad was now selling insurance to many of the school staff. In 1950, the Morris was sold and replaced with a nice Buick. He kept a tommy-gun in the back.

Dodo's replacement was, like many of the younger teachers in those days, not long out of the services. Captain Oates he was called, "Porridge" being his usual appellation among the pupils. Having fought for five years against the might of the Reich, it was obvious he was going to come down hard on the Huttites and the mayhem they created. However, we had friends in high places, one of them being the Rev MacFadzeon, Minister of the Aald Kirk, who in his spare time doubled as our Religious Instruction teacher. As I grew bigger, I came for whatever reason to resemble the Rev. more and more, until this became a joke among the guys in my class. He was always a bit ill at ease when we were in his room, especially when I started calling him Daddy. In those days folk expected a Church of Scotland minister to be a pillar of Christian manliness, and that did not include extra-marital activities of any kind. Changed days, as they say.

One day after class, he took me aside for a man to man chat. He wanted me to do my best to scotch these ill-founded rumours he said, and he knew I had the means to persuade my fellow pupils to desist. In exchange, he said, he was going to give me a useful piece of advice. Capt Oates, he said, meant to stamp out our protection racket. We'd be expelled from school and, if enough parents could be persuaded to testify, there'd be a court case. Some quick adjustment the Rev. suggested, would provide us with an escape route. The Huttites should reclassify themselves as a religious sect, and the payments being extracted from fellow pupils would then become donations by members to charitable causes. Given my co-operation, he would be prepared to vouch for this when called upon to do so, and state categorically that the Huttites were like the Quakers or the Jehovah's Witnesses and ought not to be persecuted even if they had, out of youthful enthusiasm, seemed to be a bit forceful at times. Surely, he would say, it was better for our young folk to be actively engaged in such a movement than spending their time and money on vice. "Have we got a deal, Herbie?" asked the Rev.

"A fiver says we have," I replied.

He reached for his wallet.

"A month," I interjected.

"A fiver a month!" expostulated the Rev. "I can't afford that! We ministers get very small wages!"

"You get to take platefuls of money off the folk every Sunday," I said. "Besides, you should have thought of that in the first place."

He glared at me. "I'll have to think about it," he said and sloped off. Eventually, he settled for a lump sum, which allowed me to buy my first motor bike, an ex-Army Norton 500H, just in time for me to take my first girl friend, Maisie Makelove, out on trips to interesting places in the countryside. After that, it all settled down nice and peaceful. Porridge soon found other things requiring his attention.

Just to finish this section, I'll mention a few more of the fine teachers we had thenadays. Miss Peatrose from Bressay – she was one of the Gerdie Peatroses – was our French Teacher. A more useless skill than learning French would have been hard to imagine, and we let her know it freqently. Fortunately, to get a bit of peace, she let us play cards most of the time in her room and this soon led to the setting up of a profitable poker school, which we looked forward to profiting from every day. Eventually she went off to Rhodesia and we used some of the takings to buy her a Fair Isle jersey.

Then there was "Snotterin' Bob" our woodwork and metal work teacher, who allowed us to make anything we wanted in his department. One of my brothers, Chookie, had a good line in replica SS daggers which he had no difficulty in selling to fellow pupils. I myself was not much use at these subjects, but after all my ill-fated attempts at table lamps, bedside cabinets and book cases had crashed in bits – to the delight of my classmates – Snotterin' would often send me down the Street on a "Nature Walk", which included buying him fags and a Racing Post at Connochie's. "Take your time, Herbie!" he would shout after me, and I did. I would go into the Blessed Assurance office and see if there were any letters to post and generally make myself useful. Ertie was now on the Town Council and big contracts were heading our way if he played his cards right. Competition was also hotting up, however, especially with Joyboy's Insurance, an outfit run by Tommy "Empty Chair" Johnson in Mounthooly Street. That was one reason Dad kept the tommy-gun handy in the back of the Buick. It's true what Karl Marx said: "Wherever you get poor people, you'll get insurance men."

My best subject at school was, I suppose, Maths, taught by "Chuntering Charlie" Marshall whom most of my chums found dead boring. He did go on a bit I suppose, but I must say I got a fair bit of quiet satisfaction out of his subject, either doing the simple, straightforward "summy-wummies" as Chuntering called them, or the more abstruse mathematical problems. Also, unlike the more airy-fairy subjects, your answers were either right or wrong, and your total of marks for each day's work left you in no doubt about how well, or badly you'd done compared to the rest. I have to confess I liked to get top marks, not that I got them very often.

English, taught by a guy from Unst who was a bit of a prima donna, was, in my opinion a complete waste of time. I mean, we already spoke English before we came to school, or what passed for English in this part of the country, and if you learned to speak "proper" English people would chuck stuff at you and call you a pretentious pansy, or words to that effect. Anyway, who said one sort of English is more "proper" than any other?

History I quite liked, having already learned all those dates in the Primary school. It was taught by a mad old woman called Aggie "Ding

Dong" Bell. Strict she certainly was and belted just about everyone on a daily basis, just to keep her hand in, but once she got fired up about something – like Robert the Bruce or Edward the Hammer of the Scots – she really gave it wellie and held your attention, in fact gripped your attention, till she finished. She also took the girls' hockey and ran the Drama Club after school, but that was strictly for jessies.

Science I never made much of: it should have been exciting but it was totally boring the way they did it. Our Science teacher was called "Wicked Arnott," which caused some of the more timid first year pupils to suppose he was a bad lad in his spare time and led a life of debauchery, whereas in fact he lived a completely respectable existence. His nickname was due to a keen Bible scholar finding the words "The wicked are not so…" in Psalm l. Mr Arnott was ever thereafter called "The wicked Arnott." I don't suppose today's scholars would come up with appellations quite as erudite as that for their mentors.

Art, well I have to confess I actually liked Art, although, it was reckoned pretty effeminate. My brother Bazz once told the art teacher to his face: "Ah hate Art!" The head Art guy was a fat man with a wee pointy beard. He was the first guy I ever saw wearing a velvet jacket. What a jessie! He was supposed to be a good artist in his spare time, painting pretty pictures of Shetland and stuff. Mr Small his name was. We called him "Minute" (My Newt). But what made Art both acceptable and fascinating to rough types like Yours Truly was Mr Small's assistant teacher, a young lady just out a college called Miss Whitethigh. Boy! Was she something! The big lads were putty in her hands, and we would have sat there drawing all day as good as gold, fervently hoping that at the end of the lesson, Miss W. would shimmy across to us, smile sweetly and say she thought our work was really rather interesting. If that happened, it made your day.

CHAPTER 3: I JOIN THE PANSIES.

As I was now fourteen, it was time for me to leave school and get a job. Schools took no part in this process then, which was probably just as well as most teachers only become teachers because they can't think of anything else to do. Snotterin' Bob would ask us sometimes what we were thinking of doing, and he would maybe advise you about anything he knew about in the woodwork or metalwork line. I had a half-baked notion to be a doctor as it seemed like money for jam. I've no idea how I came by it and, of course, like other teenage fantasies it was totally unrealistic, as you needed to go to the High School for that and get yourself a load of Highers, or so I'd heard. I didn't even know what Highers were, and neither did anyone else in our family. So I never mentioned this to Snotterin,' and the first job I got was a message boy with D. and C.'s grocers in Commercial Street. I got a bike with a big basket in a frame on the front, loaded this up with stuff ordered by customers, and pedalled off around town to deliver it. Once I got into the way of it and got to know some of the customers, I would try and sell them some Blessed Assurance as well, not without modest success. Dad would give me two bob for every new policy sold. My greatest achievement in this line was selling old Hughina Hughson a life insurance for her budgie.

After two years of this, Magnie Moar, the foreman in the back shop where all the goods were stored, offered me a job as a junior assistant store keeper at an extra sixpence a week. At least you got in out of the rain for part of the day, but not all day for my chief job was to go down to the Victoria Pier with a big barrow and take up stuff that had keen delivered to the steamer store off the Clair. Tea chests, cwt. sacks of meal, sugar, flour, boxes of biscuits,

At the grocers

soap, cases of wine and spirits, beer etc, not forgetting the big 45 gallon drums of paraffin which had to be rolled up to the back shop and set up on a frame and a tap screwed into them to allow folk to fill their flasks. Everyone needed paraffin in those days. This was good, healthy work for a strong, young fellow, and there was always the prospect if you did your job conscientiously and didn't cheek the boss, that you could one day become a shop man in the front shop. The downside was I didn't get to sell insurance pushing a barrow all day. Most of my spare time was spent horsing around on the Norton: it maybe wasn't always licensed, but it was definitely insured.

 At eighteeen, you got your Call-Up papers and went along to the Fort to sign up for the National Service, unless you could get it postponed by proving you were training to be a doctor or an apprentice or something. Soon we were off on the Clair to Aberdeen, my first visit to the Scottish mainland. Dad had a brother in the Granite City, but unfortunately he had recently been transferred to Peterhead to serve the remainder of his sentence. Soon we were on the train – another first for me – and heading for the big reception camp outside Stoke Wenlock in sunny England. Here we got kitted out, were provided with a number – essential in the Army – and commenced our training, which consisted mainly of marching up and down, endlessly cleaning and polishing things, and eating food any decent pig would have thought twice about. We were in the tender care of Corporal Strangeboys, a man with a unique talent for finding fault, and who generally addressed us as "Youse scum". The wooden huts were freezing cold but everything in them shone like glass. Anyone who failed to have his kit bulled up to the highest shine or

Corporal Strangeboys

who stacked his blankets a fraction squint, or maybe left his toothbrush on the wrong part of his locker top, got a spell in the punishment block, cleaning out the latrines, peeling mountains of spuds or sweeping the floor with a toothbrush. No matter how perfectly dressed you were, Cpl. Strangeboys could find a fault, and could, I am sure, have found faults in H.M. the Queen, the Pope or even Jesus Himself, and had them down on their hands and knees whitewashing coal in the supply shed. It was comforting to know that the security of the nation in that nuclear age was in the hands of such men.

I made a few chums among the lads there, such as "Little Miss" Moffat, a country boy from somewhere totally remote in Dumfriessshire who had even less of a clue than I did myself, and Guiseppe – "Big Jo" – Giorgione, a Liverpool Catholic who insisted on keeping a luminous, plastic statuette of the Blessed Virgin standing on his locker top, contrary to regulations. Eventually he obtained permission for this, though not before doing six weeks in jankers and having the C.O. beaten up by hit-men outside a tearoom in Stoke Wenlock. We were all in the same boat really, most of us, except Big Jo maybe, lacking knowledge of the big wide world, some coping better than others and all of us seriously short of cash. We were paid a pound a week in theory but there were many deductions and not even in those far off days could the remains of a quid get you much of a knees up on those weekends we were allowed out for a day in the big city of Stoke Wenlock, with all its attractions, temptations and snares of the Evil One. In fact, Stoke Wenlock was one of the dreariest dumps I have ever had the opportunity of visiting. There were a few mournful pubs patronised by dour, resentful natives, most still with sawdust on the floor, and two cafes with juke boxes. That was about the lot. The females weren't up to much either! I wasn't the only one who found it difficult to understand what they were saying. Not that they said much.

Fortunately or unfortunately, there were no other Shetlanders in the camp at that time. I say fortunately because it seems to me that whenever Shetland folk are furth of their native isles they seek out and cling fast to the company of fellow Shetlanders, sticking together like limpets on an old rock whether it's abroad on holiday, or at University or just anywhere at all. They then spend their every available moment getting up to date with all the minutiae and trivia from home, and pay very little heed at all to wherever it is they've come to. My sister Rosie eventually went to train as a Primary teacher in Aberdeen and, as she said herself, when she came back after three years there she knew far more about Bixter than Aberdeenshire because she'd chummed up with a Bixter lass there on day one. And if they can't find Shetlanders they look for Orcadians.

After six weeks of the marching up and down, we bade a tearful farewell to Cpl. Strangeboys as we were posted to our regiments, all ready to serve the nation in its hour of need as battle-ready regulars! I joined the distinguished ranks of the 2nd Battalion, Princess Augusta's North Scottish Infantry (PANSIES), and seven days later found myself in Paderborn, West Germany. Here we were issued with kilts and string vests – the PANSIES had always been a kilted regiment – in which to withstand the massed military might of the Soviet Union, which was expected to be with us any day soon. Just how a few men in kilts were supposed to succeed where the serried ranks of the Führer's Wehrmacht and Waffen SS had failed wasn't my worry. Meanwhile, I was detailed to learn machine-gunning, the first sensible skill I'd had the chance to

Pansies on Parade.

acquire since joining. As my Dad said later, if I ever thought of joining the insurance business, this could come in handy. Of course, it's different nowadays.

Life was a bit more energetic in Paderborn than it had been in sunny Stoke. Exercises – manoeuvres – took the place of marching about all day. Large parts of north Germany are covered with bleak moorland, a bit like Caithness, ideal tank country they said, and here we spent weeks biffing each other in simulated invasion scenarios. Red Force was the Russians – imaginative or what? – and White Force was the goodies. The PANSIES 2nd Battalion was an armoured reconnaissance outfit they told us – not that many of us were much the wiser – which apparently meant our job was to scout around in front of the main army, bringing back information and the occasional prisoner, whilst at the same time, of course, defending ourselves as we would inevitable encounter enemy reconnaissance units up to similar tricks from Red Force. This was good fun, especially grabbing Red Force guys and taking them back, bound and gagged, kicking and screaming, to White Force HQ, where they were "interrogated" by our officers. I suppose my early years prowling around Lerwick housing estates and jumping on other kids in the dark stood me in good stead for this. I organized a group of four of us who came to specialise in this type of work and at the end of three months I was promoted to Lance Corporal. L/Cpl Voar! Can you imagine? Boy! Was I proud! I couldn't wait for World War Three to start so's I could bring in Soviet captives for interrogation. Capt. Truehart, who was i/c Interrogations for the 2nd Batt. was impressed. "That Voar chep is as keen as mustard," he remarked one day to our CSM.

Before I fully understood what was happening, I was packed off on a course to Bad Homburg. "This course," explained the Instructor, a muscle-bound Adonis, who kept flexing his fingers on a lump of putty which he would throw at any of us without warning, and expect you to catch it, "is for keen types." We looked around at the others to see what keen types looked like, if they were different from just ordinary types. "If you are still keen at the end of this intensive course, then you can be sure there is a place for you in the modern British Army." "Golly," I thought. "What's all this about?"

It began with a course in Unarmed Combat, followed by Silent Killing, then Basic Russian, which was the one I didn't enjoy. Silent Killing was a doddle, mainly about the best ways to garotte someone with a bit of piano wire. We then went on some hands-on experience, when each of us was pitted against lethal types who'd already passed the course and come through with flying colours. All of this was done in full combat kit, including about a hundredweight of stuff on your back, black balaclavas, heavy equipment, not forgetting the piano wire. And as well as all that there was the machine gun and hand grenades. It was pretty heavy going and some dropped out after a while, but I stuck to it. Silent Killing was my

idea of fun. "When do we get to do this for real on the Russkis, Sarge?" I asked the Instructor. "Soon enough, Sonny," was his reply. "The balloon could go up any day." Some didn't like that idea at all. Others, including myself, couldn't wait. "Roll on World War Three!" was our idea.

The course lasted six exhausting weeks, ending with a test, partly practical and partly written, this being mostly about elementary Russian. I thought I was bound to fail. Never in my life had I ever passed any sort of written exam, let alone one in a foreign language. I couldn't even write English properly. Fortunately we had a coach who put in a lot of hours making us learn a fair amount parrot-fashion until gradually we began to acquire a little confidence. On the big day he wished us luck and told us that if we passed, we'd be promoted. This made all of us do our very best. Three passed. I was one. I'd actually passed an exam in elementary Russian! I couldn't believe it and was completely overjoyed. Two days later the three of us were Corporals, and heading for a suitable celebration down the rough end of Bad Homburg.

CHAPTER: 4. WITH JOCK FORCE IN THE JUNGLE

Shortly after this momentous event, I was given a fortnight's leave. I got a free trip in an Army plane to Gatwick and a ticket to the nearest railway station to Shetland, Thurso in Caithness, which was very handy. At this time, Mother's brother Uncle Osea Wonook was starting to doit, so me and my brother Chookie, who was an apprentice painter and decorator decided – after heavy hints from Mother – to go up to Mid Yell and help him with his voar. Osea's wife Hughina looked after us and we cast peat, delled the rigs, planted spuds, checked all their ewes, scraped and painted Osea's boat, the Rhubarb Queen, and generally got things in decent order for the start of another year. Auntie Hughina was a Banks from Fetlar – one of the Blue Banks – and they had four children, now all grown up. Betsy was a nurse in the Gilbert Bain, Maryline was a stewardess on the Soothboat, Dolomina was on the crew of the Morning Glory, working out of Peterhead, and Norabelle was still at home helping about the croft. Mid Yell in those days was a very hospitable place. It was still officially "Dry" so if you wanted a dram you had to get yourself either to Burravoe, to Mackie Hughson's shop there, or to the Greenbank shop in Cullivoe. There was a constant trickle of men bound for these two life-enhancing spas. Money was in short supply as jobs were almost non-existent. VP Wine was the main drink, not because it was good, but because it was the cheapest drink you could get. I don't think there was any Buckfast in those days, not thereabouts anyway. Transport was hard to come by as well. Ancient motor cycles were the vehicles most often seen, although cars – usually depooperit wrecks on their last legs and sold cheap to Yell men because there was no MOT there – were slowly increasing. I was not long in discovering Uncle Osea's long disused Triumph 350 parked in the old byre and wasted no time overhauling it and readying it for action. Soon, Chookie and I were able to chug off to Burravoe for some essential supplies. Those were the days all right. Not quite the same as Silent Killing maybe, but not without their attractions, foremost among which were two Burravoe ladies we became acquainted with during our short but memorable agricultural holiday. Maybe Chookie got better acquainted than I did, for before very long he decided to get married to his Burravoe lass, Thomasina Norie, one of the Foula Nories, which pleased Dad once he got over his initial reluctance to see young Chookie take on the weighty responsibilities of wedded bliss, (and fatherhood). He still had two years of his apprenticeship to serve, so money was tight and they had to live at No. 8 Provost Freebie Drive. Those were the days.

Me + Chookie heading for Broch.

Naturally, on my return to Paderborn, I was keen to start putting my new-found, language skills at the nation's disposal, and had been unofficially promised a posting to the Battalion interrogation unit, in which I envisaged myself interrogating captured Russian prisoners, beating them about the head with a bit of hosepipe, and maybe selling them some insurance while I was about it. Alas, however, it was not to be. The army, I soon learned, did not work quite like that. No sooner was I settled in than orders came for the PANSIES to prepare for active service in Magongoland, a British Crown colony in central Africa where, it appeared, they were having a bit of an "Emergency" – in other words, bloody mayhem had broken out, the natives were demanding independence and the Governor, Sir Evelyn Truscott-Farbelow, had been ambushed and shot.

Soon, we found ourselves sweltering on the runway at Windsor, the capital, still in our thick winter kit as there had been, as usual, "a bit of a hold-up" with the appropriate tropical supplies. As all our training had been in North Germany, we found ourselves a bit clueless on our first jungle forays, though things improved a bit once we got the correct light weight kit. The trouble was, of course, that the natives were fighting on their home turf, so basically they could come and go as they pleased

Death of Sir Evelyn Truscott-Farbelow.

and generally make circles round us. Our numbers started to dwindle. Crawling through the jungle trying to locate rebel units was fairly hard work. Vicious insects bit you, injected you with lethal poisons or entered various parts of your anatomy to give you a rough old time. I contracted dysentry and was moved back to the King George V Hospital, Windsor where, by good luck, I met Maisie Manson from Mossbank, who was working there as a nurse. She soon had me up and running again, especially after a bowl of her reestit mutton soup.

I meet Mary Manson from Mossbank

Meanwhile Major Truehart, now our CO, had received intelligence to the effect that the rebels – or "Marxist-Leninist Freedom Fighters" as they called themselves – were receiving support through a Russian military legation in the neighbouring Belgian enclave of Upswapo. This made it a bit more serious than a tribal uprising. As a reconnaissance unit it was our job to find out more. The Major therefore formed a small Special assault Group (SAG) comprising a few of our lads and some men from the Royal Magongoese Rifles (RMR) who were to be dropped up-country by helicopter, behind rebel lines. They were to live off the land and work on their own except for minimal radio contact. I was one of those chosen. In charge of the unit, known as "Jock Force," was Capt. "Mad Jock" Gorbals-Fieldfare, a very good man. Here at last, in the middle of the African jungle, my elementary Russian might come in handy.

Capt. "Mad Jock" Gorbals-Fieldfare

This was one of the roughest escapades in my young life since chucking World War 2 hand grenades into folk's houses on dark nights in Lerwick. Our chums from the RMR proved a godsend as they were already thoroughly acquainted with life in the jungle, and under their tuition and suitably blacked up, we now managed to blend in fairly well with our lush environment. Captain Gorbals-Fieldfare and his RMR equivalent, Lt. "Bonzo Dog" Doodah-Banda, planned to biff the enemy where it would hurt most. We constructed simple native-type canoes, launched ourselves on the turgid waters of the great, grey green greasy Urumguano River and set off paddling energetically with the current behind us, making good speed except when one of our craft ran aground on a submerged hippo. The lads were tipped out into the waters but were otherwise unharmed. At night we camped on the river bank to the chirping, grunting, screeching and roaring of the myriad beasts and insects of the those regions. A bit like a Saturday night in Lerwick.

After about a week of this, the Urumguano had widened considerably, and we paddled into Upswapo and beached the canoes on the swamp-infested shore among the ramshackle jetties of the trading town of Rumbaba, capital of the territory. Here we merged easily with the natives, and it did not take us long to locate the heavily fortified USSR "Trade Mission" as they called it, in the main drag, Leopold Boulevard. Plainly, Capt Gorbals-Fieldfare's plan called for considerable ingenuity, but we had not come empty-handed. Between the lot of us we had enough explosives to blow up half of Brussels. Lt. Bonzo had a sister, Maria, living and working in Rumbaba as a … er … night club hostess. She ensured we had a cosy corner in their premises to doss down about the nights and prepare for our effort. Not only that but she also secured us a decent get-away vehicle. This was not the only providential discovery in Rumbaba, for who should I find living there but Geordie Halcrow from Dunrossness, my Mother's cousin, who was teaching English at the Jesus Saves Mission. Geordie had some slight difficulty believing I was who I said I was for I was completely blacked up and wearing native-type apparel. Once we got talking however about all the folk and places we knew, his doubts disappeared and we had a great night, ending up back at Maria's. It was really great sitting there with a few beers in that strange location and blethering away non-stop in Shetland patois. The ladies took us for Russians. Geordie even told me that his boss, Rev. Moses Mbeki, had a brother married to a woman from South Festing, Lizzie Jarmson, Charlie Jarmson's sister, who used to be the first mate on the old south boat. Their father, Magnie, was a cousin of my Dad's auntie Vyra who lived in Papa Stour for a while before emigrating to Australia about the same time as Geordie came to Africa. Geordie thought Vyra had at least five children after that, but her man left her and he didn't know what happened after that, although he thought at least one of them had returned to Shetland and was living in Walls and had a job as a social worker in Foula, not a job for the faint-hearted. In fact I discovered later that Aunty Vyra had trained as a pilot and was working with Quantas, flying regular flights between Queensland and South East Asia.

Jock Force's Zero Hour was now upon us, an hour before dawn the following morning. Capt Gorbals-Fieldfare hadn't told any of us when it would be, so that none of us could blab it to anyone else. I had a bit of a headache from the night before, but I am proud to say it did not prevent me from lobbing grenades accurately into the two pillboxes at the fortified entrance gates of the "Trade Mission." That's when the fun started. From the pillboxes we bombarded the main block with bazookas, then ran across the courtyard without let or hindrance to occupy the two side wings where we knew from previous reconnaissance that the main bods were located. Meanwhile, the central block blazed merrily out of control. We'd taken the Russkis entirely by surprise. First Secretary Smolensk was still fast asleep when our lads interrupted his slumbers, and KGB General Betrzelkova, a lady not wholly unlike Aald Leebie in bodily form, whilst certainly fully awake and blazing away with her AK 47, was brought down by a rugby tackle by Lt Bonzo, who had acquired this skill – he later told me – on an officer's training course at Sandhurst.

Meanwhile Capt Gorbals-Fieldfare and I had gone through their office files and extracted handfuls of random bumf, stuffing it all into his haversack and hoping it would supply some conclusive proof of Soviet Involvement in the Magongo Emergency.

After lobbing a few more grenades into the remaining quarters, it was time to make ourselves scarce, bearing Comrades Smolensk and Betrzelkova among us, trussed up like chickens and gagged appropriately. It still wasn't daylight although the explosions and massive blaze had awakened many of the inhabitants all around, and the local fire brigade was already there. Maria had secured a decent minibus for our getaway and we were soon roaring down Leopold Boulevard, heading for the swamp-infested river banks, an environment that would, we hoped, hold up any pursuit. Here, to our joy, we found that Capt Gorbals-Fieldfare had managed to purloin a motor launch, which meant we would not now be paddling like hell, all the way up the mighty Urumguauo against the current. Soon we had left behind the sleazy delights of Rumbaba – regretfully, it must be said – while the sun rose on a scene of considerable British chaos.

CHAPTER 5: SERGEANT VOAR ON PARADE.

That launch was a temperamental and elderly lady, breaking down on several occasions on our lengthy journey upriver, though between our lads and Lt Bonzo's, we had a few experts capable of keeping the thing going in the right direction. Eventually, the river narrowed and shoals and dense overhanging green stuff made further motorised progress impossible. We had to get out and walk. Apart from natural obstacles we were still behind enemy lines, so to get back to Windsor, Magongoland, we would either infiltrate our way skilfully and silently through their lines, or attack them at the earliest opportunity and attempt to bulldoze our way through. Either way we'd need luck.

I suppose what determined Capt Gorbals-Fieldfare on the second course was the continual insults of our Soviet chums, whose gags had been removed to ensure they didn't suffocate during the exhausting process of crawling through the stifling undergrowth. Every ten minutes or so, one or the other would assure us that we were certain to fall into the hands of the Marxist-Leninist Freedom Fighters, who would then make sure we all died excruciating and protracted deaths in return for our treatment of two of the Soviet Union's finest. After listening to variations of this message for three days on end, the captain decided he'd show them exactly what would happen to their Marxist-Leninists when faced with the combined might of the PANSIES and the RMR. He wasn't called "Mad Jock" for nothing. Easier, perhaps, would have been to shoot the two Russians, but he meant to hand them over alive and well to the authorities in Windsor as proof of the USSR's involvement in the internal affairs of Magongoland.

Maps of this area were sketchy at best. There were no roads, the river was now unnavigable, and only a few "native villages" were marked, some of them with Question Marks. Some villages were known to be in guerrilla hands: others were of uncertain loyalty. Once again, we could probably not have done much without Lt Bonzo's expertise and that of his men, some of whom were expert trackers.

Six days out from the river we entered the remote jungle village of Uluwagga, where several of Lt Bonzo's men had relatives. We were no sooner there than we were surrounded by welcoming natives bearing trays of fruit, and ladies with basins of water to wash our weary feet. After six days of hot slog it was as good as a rest cure. They really treated us well there: the partying began that evening and went on for days thereafter, I'm not certain how many exactly. Our Soviet chums were decidedly dischuffed: these people gave little sign of wanting to overthrow their imperialist oppressors and embrace the joys of Marxism-Leninism. Better than that, they had accurate knowledge of the whole area for many miles around. We could have slipped through enemy lines, no bother, but Capt Gorbals-Fieldfare was determined to biff the opposition now he had the chance.

After a week in Uluwagga, we were in pretty decent shape: well fed, rested and keen to show 'em our appreciation of their hospitality by smiting the enemies of Uluwagga. Slowly, silently we edged our way through the Jungle behind our native guides, making for the ML headquarters, a large village called Chumumba. Night was falling when we reached it, with its red flag hanging limply from a pole outside a compound of native buildings surrounded by a stockade. Now we settled down for the night: pre-dawn assaults were apparently Capt Gorbals-Fieldfare's speciality. Few of us got much sleep, thanks to the insect life and the howls and twitterings from the undergrowth. There were also snakes.

One hour before dawn as was his custom, the gallant Captain blew his little whistle and we lobbed our grenades into the sleeping compound. Then we opened up with the bazookas. All hell broke loose. The MLs were heavily armed with Soviet weaponry, but having been sound asleep, they started at a distinct disadvantage and never really recovered. About two hundred would never fire a Kalashnikov again, and the rest fled into the jungle.

It was a major victory for British and RMR guts, determination and drive – with apologies to any trendy or politically correct readers who may suffer an attack of the vapours reading such outmoded language. Not long afterwards, and safely back in base, Major Truehart had us parade through Windsor to the skirl of the pipes, when eight of us were presented with suitable medals and all were commended in the despatches of the day. Before the end of the year, I had another stripe on my arm: Sgt. Voar at your service, Sah!

Major Truehart dishes out the gongs

CHAPTER 6: ON LEAVE.

Although our jungle friends the Marxist-Leninists had suffered a serious setback, and the proven complicity of the USSR caused an international stushie at the time, the Emergency was still alive and kicking. Comrades Smolensk and Betrzelkova, after a long interrogation were eventually put on a plane to Moscow – where they were soon shot. A new Governor, Brig Gen Sir Fennimoore Barking-Thrush, MC, KT, arrived with instructions to prosecute the fight with the utmost vigour, and as our lads were now a lot more experienced, we were only too willing to oblige. It was either that or patronise the Windsor night life, and although that certainly had its attractions, vigorous campaigning aginst the MLs was probably a lot healthier and certainly a lot less expensive. I may add in passing, modestly I hope, that there was at this time, in one of the two main entertainment districts of Windsor, an establishment known as "Voar's 'Ores."

Many guys of my acquaintance who did National Service complained ever after that it was boring and pointless. I certainly did not find this. Not only was it full of exciting opportunities, but I'd already upped my modest income by gaining promotion more than once. It wasn't possible for a National Serviceman to rise higher than the rank of Sergeant. This was one of the factors I took into consideration when, in due course, Capt Gorbals-Fieldfare suggested to me I might like to extend my service by another three years and go for a Short Service Commission. He was also good enough to say I was the sort of "chep" the Army was always glad to get: I had the right attitude, didn't hang back when action was required and generally had the makings of someone who could, given the right training, lead and enthuse other ranks. I know he was only saying his piece, but I have to say I took it as a bit of a compliment, considering my humble background. I decided to go for it. I mean, opportunities of advancing in life were as likely to come my way as gold bars. Besides, it's not as if I didn't have any brothers and sisters to help with the various chores and duties at home or in Mid Yell, where Uncle Checkie had recently died. Chookie and Thomasina – and wee George – had already decided to move there and take over the croft.

Home reactions to my decision were, as you'd expect, mixed. Mother thought I'd only get myself killed by nasty black men. Dad seemed to think I'd do a lot better coming home as soon as my two years were up and joining Blessed Assurance. He claimed business was booming, but there really wasn't much booming business anywhere in Shetland in the 'Fifties and early 'Sixties. Everyone was skint. The smart ones were going to university to get qualified, and even then, you needed to be in an Old Pals' Clique to get any sort of decent job in Shetland. That never changes. Others, including just about every able-bodied man in Yell, had gone off to the whaling, courtesy of Salvesens. Between that and another three years in the PANSIES, I knew which I'd prefer. Nowadays, however, I'm not so sure. The whaling was little better than slavery in very poor conditions, but at least you saved some money. In the army, all your pay went down your throat.

The Plan, as the new Governor explained it, was three-pronged. We were Prong One: continuing to biff the MLs with maximum vigour. Prong Two consisted of finding out from prisoners or any other source exactly what were the rebels' real grievances. If it was all just the standard Lefty Claptrap – as Sir Fennimoore phrased it – then we had nothing more to learn. But if there were any real grievances, then it was his intention, he said, to do something to alleviate them, and so remove their causes of grievance.

Prong Three: a General Election would be held – the first ever in Magongoland – to result in a chamber of deputies from among whom he would choose a governing council, thus, he hoped, at least demonstrating the administration's willingness to institute democratic rights and institutions. More, he hoped, would follow from this. The main thing was to get stuck in.

I realise that Shetland readers are unlikely to be interested in reading about constitutional development in Magongoland – or indeed anything else apart from Shetland and Shetlanders – so I shall abbreviate this. Over the next two years, Sir Fennimoore's Plan began to work. There were inter-tribal rivalries that needed sorting out, grievances that he could rectify and support to be won by open and fair government action. We hammered the MLs all the time, and so, between us and the Governor, they dwindled and lost some support. In the end the main group took refuge in the Congo. The Governor's biggest hit was undoubtedly the Election: it went off with great enthusiasm and the resultant People's Representatives brought new vigour into what had been perhaps an out-of-date colonial régime. When he retired the following year, Sir Fennimoore was elevated to the peerage, becoming Lord Barking-Thrush of Bexhill.

Not for the first or last time, my leave brought me down to earth with a bump. No one in Provost Freebie Drive was the least impressed with my sergeant's stripes, and none of my old mates seemed all that interested in tales of derring do in the jungle, apart from a few gory details. Soon it was all forgotten about as I got up to speed with the latest minutiae of an intensely parochial community. The weirdest story now was that huge quantities of oil were thought to be sloshing around under the North Sea, and that Shetland would be at the centre of any effort to get it out of there. Would there be jobs? Plenty, said the optimists. We'll all be rolling in money. It took a bit of believing.

CHAPTER 7: BOOMTIME IN UPSWAPO.

I went on my officers' course and got through it with a lot of effort. I was in two minds about a lot of it. Being a sergeant had suited me fine: decent pay and you were at the same level as most of your mates and they knew you could hack it when the fighting started. But an officer, of course, is a different breed entirely and no way one of the lads. However, as Capt Gorbals-Fieldfare put it, the army was trying to democratise its own structure by promoting more men who were not members of the traditional officers' élite. I saw his point, and that was one reason I went ahead with it: I mean, there's no point moaning about officers being all snobs and toffs if no one takes the opportunity to alter the system when they have the ball at their feet. Naturally, it was the written papers that just about scuppered my attempt: the practical parts of the course – assault courses, endurance tests etc – did not give me problems, seeing as how I'd been on an almost continuous assault course in Magongoland for a year. Another plus point was my Russian ticket. Of course, once I was through all the hoops, they posted me to Cyprus.There's a lot of Russian spoken there.

By the time of my final posting back to Magongoland, the colony's constitutional progress was bringing it within sight of future independence. For this reason the RMR was being trained for its forthcoming role as the army of a newly emergent nation, as they called it at that time. I was seconded to help forward this process, and was lucky enough to be attached most of the time to the future C in. C, Gen "Bonzo Dog" Doodah Banda, with whom I'd already served in the "Jock Force" campaign.

It was during this last part of my service that Gen Banda suggested that some of the guys from the old jungle assault group might care for a return trip to Upswapo, now that the fighting had died down. There had, he said been a lot of changes out that way, including a newly laid road across country, part of the Barking-Thrush pacification programme, and anyway, continued the General, he reckoned Maria and her girls would be very pleased to see us all again. Who would refuse an offer like that?

The new road was rough, but one very big improvement on crawling through the bug-infested swamp. We got most of the way in army lorries, plus a river ferry down part of the great grey green greasy Urumguano. We were in Rumbaba after three days.

Upswapo was a changed place all right. Vast diamond deposits had been found in the tiny territory. Massive building works were in progress all across town: hotels, office blocks, air port and public amenities were springing up all over the place. Last time we'd been there it had been slow-moving, a traditional native trading post: now the place was swarming with foreigners from every part of the globe. Vast earth-moving machinery crawled everywhere, clawing out foundations, clearing away the simple flimsy dwellings of the old town. In fact, the only place we saw in Rumbaba that hadn't been rebuilt ten times bigger was the Soviet Trade Mission: that was still in the state we'd left it.

Boomtime in Upswapo

We checked into a flash new hotel, the Intercontinental Splendide, and after a wash and brush up and a quick meal, we sauntered out into the tropic night for a visit to Maria's. Naturally, with Rumbaba now the rest and recreation capital of the whole surrounding diamond industry, the joint was jumpin' with big beefy guys with plenty cash and all looking for a good time. Maria's night club, like the others, was no longer a modest establishment in an unlit back alley: it had glitter, it had a large flashing neon frontage. Obviously as a General's sister, the proprietress wasn't going to be left behind in the rush to get rich quick, but it should be mentioned also that, despite all the flash, Maria remained a good Catholic, and her establishment was still called The Queen of Heaven Nite Club Bar, even though the flashing neon sign was about thirty feet high, and was …er… pretty explicit.

Our visit was a big success all right, but there was one unanswered question left in my mind once it all began to clear later on the next day. Was this the sort of all-encompassing change that was going to happen in dear old Shetland if the rumoured oil boom materialised?

I did another two years in the army, on top of my three, most of it in Germany. Then I left. Probably I ought to have stayed in because by then I really was making something of it. I'd been stepped up to Captain, for one thing, and I was thinking their way, no longer the off-beat, fence-sitting Shetland way. If I'd remained any longer I don't think I would ever have come back home again, unless for holidays. In other words, I'd been shaped to their mould and was ready for a good twenty years further service with the Colours, not a bad thing to be, considering. But instead, I packed it in. Dad died that Spring. He was a big man and he was going to leave a big gap. I thought it was maybe time for me to do something to fill it. Still, as Capt Gorbals-Fieldfare had often said: Once a PANSY, always a PANSY.

I spent time in London, following up several interviews. And following up a girlfriend. None of it came to anything, well nothing that need involve a lawyer. It was the height of summer. I headed back to Shetland. To tell the truth, there was only one thing I really wanted to do: get on the old Norton and go roaring off through the Isles in the fine summer weather, forgetting all the weighty responsibilities of Captain Voar. I suppose I should have had a more responsible attitude after all this time.

CHAPTER 8: BLESSED ASSURANCE BRANCHES OUT.

One man among many who was no ways impressed with what I had been doing was Ertie Spence, Cooncilor Ertie Spence, boss man of Blessed Assurance when I called, at his request, at his much enlarged premises.

"Du's been wastin' years o' dy life," he commenced without further introduction, "prancin' aboot in vainglorious wars and siclik trash. Dy faider an' me hae been extremely busy buildin' up a business, a business that noo employs seven office staff, four men poundin' da beat full time, besides a braw half dozen part-timers in various categories. We hae a lot o' Cooncil business and we're continuin' to expand despite competeetion fae Joyboys – if du could ca' it competeetion. I'd like to remind dee, Herbie, o' two tings. One, dy faider pit da best years o' his life intil dis business. And Two, it was an Ermy man, Captain Spalding, wha provided dy faider an' me wi' aal da essentials and qualifications to start up. Dat wis while da whole lok o' wis wis locked awa under da heel o' da jackboot. It wisna aesy, Herbie ma mannie, an' it's never been dat aesy since. We wis total ootsiders in Lerook business circles when we first started, but noo by oor ain efforts an' honest toil we're in wi' da brickwork an' da day's no far aff when we'll hae more pull here dan ony idder business in Shetland. Aye maybe even includin' da Cooncil. Are ye ready to bend your back to da burden, Herbie Boy? For if no, I can get ye your aald job back again as storeman at D and Cs, and du can carry on there just whaur du left aff, an' rise in due course to be a shopman in da front shop. An' nothin' wrang wi' dat, I may say, for a job's a job an', as du laekly keens, they're no dat aesy to come across hereaboots."

What was he coming up with? He plainly had something on his mind, and his reference to the late Capt Spalding made it clear, despite the disparaging remarks in his introduction, that he did consider it possible I might have something to offer. I told him I was all ears.

"Ting is, Herbie," he continued, "there's more to Blessed Assurance nooandays than just insurance. Once we'd got a bit o' spare cash geddered in aboot, dy faider an' me gave some tought to da best possible uses for dat small capital, an' it didna tak wis lang to see da wey ahead: Loans. Karl Marx was right when he said: Whereever du gets poor folk, du'll aye get loan sharks. But it wisna just poor people, dat's da beauty o' it. In Shetland everyone's skint, from da humble cottar to da Loard Lieutenant

Himself, God Bless and Keep Him. Of coorse, there's da banks. But has du ever tried gettan' a loan oot o' a bank?"

"I widna daur," I said.

"Exactly!" he said. "Du'd feel better aboot bein' tortured by da Spainish Inquiseetion than bein' grilled by een o' yun starch fronts and dan rejected for haein' sic impertinence. But ordinary folk need to borrow money, Herbie, for all sorts of important things, and dat's why they need folk at their own level, and on their own doorstep. Folk like wis, Herbie. Blessed Assurance. And unlaek da banks we dinna laek turnin' doon da humble poor." (Needless to say, this was long before the era when banks went to the dogs and were actually pushing folk to take their dirty money almost without security.)

"Of coorse," Ertie continued, "we do charge a high rate of interest. Dat's becaas we tak big risks. Lendin' money is a high risk business, Herbie. In other wirds it taks guts. Like' fightin' i' da Ermy. Do I mak meself clear?"

"I get you," I said, "You need someone to go in there and kick ass. Someone who's not afraid of a bit of aggro."

"Noo du's talkin!" said Ertie, rubbing his scrawny neck with a gnarled hand.

"What sort of interest, anyway?" I asked.

"Weel," he said cagily. "It aal depends. 25% maybe, sometimes 40%. Sometimes a lot more. Depends, on hoo lang it's for, an' a variety o' other delicate matters, like just hoo desperate da punter is to get his haunds apo' da cash. Someen wha's really desperate will pay hundreds per cent just to get whit he wants, believe me. All human life is there, Herbie ma beauty. It's no just paperwork this job. Du'll meet da full gamut o' human life an' emotions as dey say: lust, greed, fear, desire, covetousness, envy, malice – an' a lot more besides. It's wir job to mak a profit from it aal. Dat's business, Herbie, an' business is da only ting dat keeps Shetland runnin'. Withoot it we'd aal be at da mercy o' da state, just laek Hitler an' Stalin wanted. Na, na, Herbie ma man, dinna let da Lefties tell du idderwise.

"Ony wey, as I said, we started small on da hoosin' estates, but since dan, tings has blossomed into some o' da more lush nooks an' crannies o' wir dear island hom. Word got aroond as aye it does in Shetland, an' we began to get da odd business man, shopkeeper an' farmin' mannie comin' to me in private, often efter Cooncil meetings. an' tellin' me hoo he needed a bit o' extra capital, an' da banks were absolutely hopeless. Maybe a shopkeeper who'd overspent on his private yacht, or a businessman who liked to visit the ladies on his trips to gay Paree, or gay Aiberdeen mair laek. The poor hae no monopoly on fecklessness, Herbie, as Karl Marx aye said. Human fecklessness is big business if you can just turn it into cash. An' dat's just as it should be. So, of coorse, they got their loans. Some o' em paid it back and mighty grateful too – dat sort o' gratitude aye helps when it comes to Cooncil contracts, of coorse. But some poor bodies alas, just got demsels deeper an' deeper intil debt. Da interest payments couldna be met. Then, Bang! It aal collapses, an dat, Herbie, to cut a long an' painful story short, is how Blessed Assurance cam to own shops in Lerook, businesses here and there, and een or twa half decent ferms oot an' aboot i'da beautiful countryside o' Shetland. Of coorse, we dinna trumpet wir modest gains from da tap o' da Toon Haal. But it's definitely a growing businesss Herbie, an aal needs careful management. We could do wi' someen wi' experience in whit dey nooandays caals man-management, to look efter these extra concerns, an (if dat someen was also da kind o' billy we meentioned earlier wha could, as du said deesel, Kick Ass when it comes to solicitin' loan repayments, then I reckon maybe dee an' me might hae someting to discuss i'da way o' appropriate remuneration, for services rendered, as Marx himsel aye said."

So that was what the cards foretold. At least I'd solved one little mystery; I now knew how Ertie had acquired his latest nickname: The Loan Ranger.

CHAPTER 9: AWAY UP NORTH.

So that's how I left the Army and became a loan shark. Like the army, the job had its seedier side, and there were also occasions where brute force had to be employed. That didn't bother me. If folk are daft enough to buy things they can't afford, they have to face the consequences. Paradoxically, this side of the business mushroomed after the oil jobs started. You might have thought that with decent pay, folk would never need to borrow, but all that happened was they got a lot greedier. The worst of it to my mind was that a lot of Shetland folk, ceased being Shetland folk, and just got down to grabbing and spending like the rest of the modern culture.

Most of my time from now on was spent managing businesses that Ertie had taken over when their owners defaulted on his loans. As businesses, some of them had only a limited life anyway: shops in Commercial Street especially. The glory days on that particular boulevard were disappearing forever as the newly affluent punters took their custom to Tin Pan Alley in Gremista. Commercial Street became the lifeless ghost walk it now is. Not that this worried Ertie in the least. The shops might be profitless, but property prices began to move up, and have been doing so ever since. As long as he could get Planning Permission for turning 'em into office blocks, pubs or Arts Venues, he was quids in. And Cooncillor Ertie never seemed to have much of a problem getting Planning Permission. Even before he became Cooncil Convenor.

Dad, of course, had now moved out of No 8 Provost Freebie Drive, so I moved back in. The house was comparatively empty, as quite a few of the other seventeen had gone their separate ways. Herkie was now in the Merchant Navy sailing the seven seas with the Blue Star Line. Bazz was in the motor trade in Aberdeen, Rosie was teaching in Boddam. Jessamine was married to peerie Joe Stove, an electrician with the Coonty: they lived up the North Road. Wee Freddie and Mop were still at school, and Chimmie was up in Mid Yell staying with Old Daa, Mother's Grandad. He was a fair age but healthy and fit as a flea. He would run five miles every day, summer and winter, and often plunged fully clothed into the Voe off the Linkshouse pier, when he thought no one was looking. Chimmie and him got on well, Chimmie being a mad beggar anyway, and when the Canning Factory started up, he got a job there and lived up at Old Daa's thereafter, helping with the croft, not that Daa needed much help. He was one of four old guys there at Mid Yell at that time who all still had the old Kitchener-type moustaches, and all of them fit and healthy. The other three were Andro Leask, Peter Clark and – maybe the doyen of them all – Addie Sandison, Altona, who was sharp as a new pin though pretty deaf by this time. I mind Peter Clark telling him once: "Addie, du's as deef as da heed o' Hivdigarth!" You could hardly get more Mid Yell as that.

Aald Daa

We had a dose of relatives up there although Mother's father, Herbert, was no longer living, and Uncle Osea Wonook had been put to the Brevik as happened in those days before they got the Isleshaven Care Centre, a great blessing to all. Chookie and Thomasina, and wee George, and wee Brianella, were up at Uncle Checkie's old croft at Ooter Gerdie, and Chookie had a job with the Coonty Road Men, a worthy band who get plenty criticism from self-styled experts on road construction but whose job maintaining roads in a place as full of deep peat as Yell is by no means easy. Mid Yell in those days at least was about the friendliest place anyone could hope to find in this world. Of course, we were biased I suppose.

But I will also say that Yell as a whole, which some seem to find dull and none too bonnie, possesses a unique, almost unearthly beauty of its own. Its colours are subtle not bright, its contours not dramatic but lithe and as it were enclosing mysteries that the rushing passer-by will never even suspect. The largest part of the island is wholly hidden from view and from the road-user's gaze. Hidden lochs, dales, deserted villages, bronze age forts, ancient burial places and coasts all presenting dramatic contrasts to the gentle folds of the hills. I daresay it's not a tourist magnet like the Costa Brava or Tenerife, but who says tourists are the supreme arbiters of beauty?

On fine weekends, I would take the Norton across on the old Shalder – the little passenger ferry on Yell Sound before the big vehicle ferries started – bike up through Yell and stop off at Old Daa's or Chookie's, then in the morning continue to Gutcher and, if there was a ferry maybe get across to Unst with Davie Johnson on the old Trystie. What a boat! And what a seaman! That was the way I came to meet Nora, da Nort Isles Woman, but the least said about that the better.

Not, of course, that this was all just about a round of pleasure: I mean, I wouldn't like anyone to think I now spent my days just bombing around. That would never do. Well, it was partly that I suppose, but partly also in the interests of business. It had struck Ertie and me that there was a sizeable potential market for our unique services at the extreme north end of Shetland, at RAF Saxa Vord in fact, Unst, where some 200 captive servicemen and their wives and families were doomed to spend two years far from the comforts and distractions of dear old England. Their overseers and taskmasters were glad to hear from anyone with a service to provide that would make their lives more fulfilling. And that, of course, was just what we were willing to do. That's just how we saw ourselves: as service providers, as they say nowadays, like travel agents, bookies or brothels. It took no time at all to fix up an interview with the CO, Wing Co. "Soppy" Sopwith-Camel, DFC and Bar, who was only too willling to allow one to leave business cards all over the premises advising the RAF lads and their good ladies that, whatever they needed by way of a little bit of extra finance was always there to hand with Blessed Assurance. We were there to see them all right. "What a good idea!" enthused the Wing Co. "I'm sure a lot of our cheps will avail themselves of your services." We soon fell to chatting about life in the armed forces, especially about Germany, where he'd also spent some time. I got the impression that the Wing. Co.

didn't just see all that many folk he could chat to in the course of a day, and the English of course, if I may say so without serious racial offence, do like to chat. If they're deprived of chat they start to feel decidedly unhappy, unlike the dour Scot – not all Scots are dour of course, it just seems like that – who doesn't give a monkey's whether he gets to chat or not, and will gladly stay shtum all year rather than chat to folk he doesn't like – which means just about everyone.

To my surprise, the CO told me he rather thought there was a chep I might know lurking at the Secondary School there, a man called Tom "Feeble" Ferris whom I'd known at Paderborn when he was a junior 2nd Lieutenant in the PANSIES. Before leaving Saxa Vord therefore, I obtained Feeble's present address and, seeing school was probably out for the day and that I still had a couple of hours to wait before the ferry, thought I'd zap along there on the Norton and look him up before returning to Yell. He certainly got a surprise when this muffled figure hurtled into his rude native compound.

"Herbie!" he exclaimed. "What on earth...?"

"I might ask the very same of yourself, Feeble old fruit," I said, "I thought you were keeping back the Red Hordes."

Feeble, it transpired, always a lad for the ladies, had had woman trouble and had left the Army in a hurry at considerable expense. Fortunately for him, his uncle, Davie Ratter from Twaxter, was on the Education Committee and was soon able to fix Feeble up with the job of knitting teacher in Unst, a job for which he was at that time not particularly well qualified, but which allowed him to keep the wolf from the door. He greatly regretted his misdeeds, he said, especially his leaving the PANSIES since he was he said, "one of Nature's Pansies," so to say he was chuffed to see a fellow ex-Pansy again is no exaggeration. He forthwith laid aside his knitting and started 'phoning around to gather a few like-minded buddies and other degenerates to make a chum welcome, having first persuaded me to cancel my ferry crossing and stay *chez* Feeble's overnight. I had heard of the exemplary hospitality in Unst: I was about to witness it at first hand.

By eight o'clock the joint was jumpin', people playing fiddles, accordians, guitars, punters of many varieties milling around and enjoying the hastily – but lavishly – provided goodies. There were crofters talking about cows, teachers moaning non-stop about all the things teachers moan

Tom "Feeble" Ferris.

non-stop about, RAF guys and their girl friends. Even Wing Co. Sopwith-Camel and his lady wife, Elvira put in an appearance, the good lady taking the opportunity to sound me out about a home loan for a modest *manoir* she was thinking of acquiring in the Dordogne. She seemed to think she'd get a better deal from the Halifax, but that little misapprehension was smoothed out before the end of the night.

About midnight, people being then generally mellow and open to suggestion, I ventured to give a brief five minute spiel about our services. You don't want to miss a trick. I pointed out that getting into debt to a Sooth bank was not helping Shetland any, when you could almost certainly raise the funds on better terms here at home from B. A. Within a week, I'd heard from five folk who wanted to know more.

You might expect a community at the furthest northern edge of Scotland to be inward looking and not particularly welcoming to strangers but Unst, as well as being spectacularly beautiful had long been used to entertaining – and making an honest living from – numerous incomers. Long before the RAF Camps – the first of these during World War 2 – the island played host to thousands of fisherfolk, male and female, who came there annually in pursuit of the great herring fishery in the late 19th and early 20th centuries. If dourness is inbred in many parts of Scotland, so too is hospitality in places like Unst. That's how I met Nora the Nort Isles Woman. When I left the next morning, I had a nice chocolate sponge in my back pack.

Of course, not all the human flotsam washed up on the shores of Britain's most northerly isle is there on official or strictly commercial business. The 'Sixties witnessed the advent of the first hippies and other nirvana seekers, some on their own just wandering about dispensing Peace and Love, Man, others in communes or other forms of sharing and caring. Among these was the notable Dr Jonathan Trot, part-time boatman and one-time Socialist, ex-Rector, Labour Party candidate, newspaper editor, Cooncillor, wildlife pundit and tour provider, author, cartoonist, the kind of comrade who in Victorian times would have gone out and colonised some faraway and thoroughly obscure part of the British Empire.

Feeble Ferris didn't do so badly either. It didn't take him long to appreciate that the old ways of sound Scottish education were gone, kaput, as the trendy Lefties and other mediocrities moved in like Butch Elm Disease. They were out to ding doon "elitism" – what we used to call High Standards – and for a kick-off they meant to scrap all traditional forms of education and replace it with entertainment. Feeble was quick to jump on this bandwagon of clowns, as the holder of an MA in Knitting and Multi Tasking from the University of Aberthicko (£200 the lot, including mortar board and free hire of graduation gown.) In no time at all he was Shetland Islands Council Education Committee's Adviser in Knitting and Textile Skills, spending his time, as all advisers do, when he wasn't generating paperwork and guide lines, out and about telling other teachers how to suck eggs. From such humble beginnings he rose in record time to Director of Education, or rather to be quite politically correct, to Manager of Education, Sport, Dog Racing and Family Planning. By then, of course, the Cooncil and its gargantuan bureaucracy, having expanded to such a bloated extent, managers of this, that and the next had become almost as common as dirt.

CHAPTER 10: AUNTY VYRA GOES TO CHURCH.

The advent of the Oil Age has had much the same effect on Shetland as diamonds had in Upswapo. Everyone scrambled to get his piece of the action, local businesses that had previously seemed fairly substantial were now seen as only quaint midgets. This was true of Blessed Assurance like all the rest: the funds Ertie and Co. had been toiling to generate since 1946 were like sweetie money compared to the hundreds of millions of pounds being sloshed around by oil companies, major banks and government departments. From being a shark in a little pond, Ertie had become a tiddler in a sea full of mighty leviathans, who could squash him without even noticing. Not that Ertie was worried. Like lawyers and brothels, the world's other oldest professions, there have always been money lenders and always will be.

No. What was worrying the man in the bow tie was: how was he – like everyone else – going to grab his piece of the oil goodies? It didn't seem likely that Shell or Grabola UK would be all that grateful for the sort of finance that solved problems on Provost Freebie Drive.

Everyone who was in Shetland during these times is well aware of the big changes. There were good results and bad. Among the good were decent jobs and proper pay. Among the worst, in my opinion, are the vastly expanded bureaucracies in every sphere of life. Bureaucracy is fascism without the jackboots. It's a system that gives huge dictatorial powers to the sort of faceless paper gauleiters who could never achieve real power by their own merit or guts. These are the same sort of persons who used in byegone days to run the late Führer's holiday camps for him: not monsters, just little faceless guys who'd go back home at the end of another successful day's gassing and put a nice waltz record on the radiogram.

Auntie Vyra had long planned to return to the land of her birth for a proper holiday, and as she spent her days flying planes between Darwin, Indonesia and PNG, as she called it, she certainly had the smackeroolas to do the job right. We'd all heard plenty over the years about this Aussie Wonder Sheila but none of us except Dad had ever seen her, so when she booked in at the recently erected Hotel Shetlandic, we were all there to give her a suitable hearty welcome. With her came her second husband, a large and taciturn hunk of East European manhood, whose communication skills were severely restricted to a combination of Balkan vocabulary and a broad Australian accent. We couldn't even fully figure out his name: it was spelled with no vowels and so many Zs, Cs and other symbols stuck all over it that only himself could pronounce it properly. Vyra called him Count Dracula. He didn't seem to mind that.

She herself spoke "Strine" like a native, loudly, and dressed and acted accordingly. Every day they went off somewhere different in a hired limo, and called in at Provost Freebie Drive on the way back to give us their opinions, before returning to the glitzy concrete luxury of their hotel. Some folk thought it was about as Shetlandic as Dubai, but others opined that it mirrored modern Shetland pretty accurately. Aunty thought it "Bonzer!"

All of which was merely preliminary to the highlight of their visit: Aunty Vyra's Return to Foula (later set to music for fiddle and didgeridoo, by J. Gear). Vyra's memories of the original Foula mail boat were such that they hired a private speed boat to get there. Once safely ashore on the mystic isle, she insisted on visiting everywhere she remembered from her childhood, including the school, church and the homes of everyone she had any connection with. When she'd done all that she set off with true antipodean energy to ascend the five peaks of this singularly mountainous isle. I don't know if Dracula managed them all: perhaps he flew part of the way. During their prolonged ascent, the natives, who had got out of bed in her honour, assembled at the new school and laid on an impromptu concert and fish supper, at which Foula's notable musicians gave of their best. Dancing, as they say, went on far into the night, and it should be recorded that despite her long and exhausting day, Aunty Vyra was still up and kicking her way through the Foula Reel till five o'clock next morning. Fortunately the weather remained calm throughout. This visit was certainly the highlight of Aunty's holiday. She seldom stopped talking about it thereafter.

On Sundays, it was Aunty's habit to go to church, and she meant, she said, to do the same here. However, as a member of the Jesus Saves Church of Latter Day Aussies, she was not going to go to just any old church, many of which, she declared, were "Backslidin' bastards, and long gone down along the Highway to Hell." I couldn't help agreeing with her, but how were we going to provide her with an acceptable worship environment, as they say nowadays? I 'phoned my dear old mentor Rev

Thomas MacFadzeon and found, to my surprise, that he had long since been ejected from his previous outfit, the C. of S. for activities I could easily guess at but had not the least desire to enquire into. I found, however, that, being a Man of God with a mission to preach the Saving Gospel of OLJC – and being also in need of a job – he had set up his own outfit called – wait for it – the Huttites! The conniving ******** had nicked our dear old gang name for his dodgy sect! This led to some impromptu telephonic exchanges, but he did point out that the Bible is full of two-timing crooks; and fornicators – in fact, it's got a lot more bad people in it than good ones, which may be why it's still read. I did eventually get around to asking him if his new congregation of Hell-deserving sinners would be a suitable shrine for a five-star sheila from the Latter Day Aussies, and his reply quickly put my mind at rest, especially after I'd told him that Aunty Vyra was no way short of the smackeroolas. "We shall be only too pleased to make the dear lady most welcome," he shmoozed.

"Not too welcome, Daddio." I advised. "Or you could have Count Dracula to deal with."

Anyway, on Sunday morning at the appointed hour I ran Aunty Vyra to the Huttites Gospel Meeting House, which in those days was about half way up Hangcliff Lane. Rev MacFadzeon was personally at the door. "G'Day Rev!" said Aunty V, wringing his flabby hand with her powerful grip. "I understand from my grand nephew, little Herbie here, that we may expect to hear some bonzer old time religion preached in this here congregation, but I'm just personally checkin' that out before I enter into the body of the kirk, so's I don't have to rise up and get the Hell outa here in the middle of the goddam service, if you get my drift, Sport."

"Let your Spirit, Dear Lady," shmoozed the pastor, hardly pausing to draw breath, "rest in peace on that matter. We preach only the Gospel of OLJC and sing only His Praises. Halleluiah! Please give generously." So saying he indicated a substantial collecting box bolted to the wall near the entrance. It had "Freely Have Ye Received: Freely Give." painted on it in big clear letters, the implication being, presumably, if you wanted the Lord to do you a few favours, make sure you paid up front. Aunty got the message and seemed thenceforth to feel at home.

On the spur of the moment, instead of waiting for Vyra at the King of Norway down the street, I decided to sit in on the service and see how dear old "Dad" was managing in this age of gross materialism to bring the punters to Jesus. I'd only ever been at a church service as a boy at Sunday School or as a soldier on church parade, but I thought that this time, as an original Huttite myself, I might some get some goodies at a reduced rate as it were.

Surprisingly, I soon found the Rev really did have a pretty persuasive style. You could see how he'd always been a hit with the ladies. It was maybe pretty nutty, but one thing it wasn't was boring. He harangued the sinners so that you really began to feel: Hey! Maybe it's me he's talking to, not just these ass****s! He praised and magnified the Lord so that you began to expect at any moment this great old guy would, like, burst through the ceiling and start welcoming repentant sinners on one side of the hall and kick the unrepentant down into Hell on the other, to the accompaniment of weeping and wailing and gnashing of teeth. Like I said, it wasn't boring, and even if you didn't really believe it, you got a good hour's spiritual provocation for your money, which you couldn't have got sitting watching the TV. Plus, you could join in the singing, which didn't do any harm either. There's no denying it made you think: could we really be held responsible for all the ass**** stuff we've done in life?

Past his best? I don't think so. His main strength was he talked in a way so's ordinary punters could follow: you didn't have to be a Bible expert or a religious nut to take his drift. That, plus, maybe, everyone knew he was a bit of an old sinner himself. I maybe shouldn't say this, but didn't OLJC have time for sinners? It seemed to me, against the odds maybe, He might also have time for the Huttites and their dodgy pastor.

I didn't have to ask Aunty if she'd approved of the service, because she'd been singing away with a will throughout, and had even started clapping her hands at one stage. "That was fair dinkum, Sport," she told MacFadzeon on the way out, giving his hand another mangling.

"Come again, Dear Lady," said the Rev. Obviously his beady eye had not failed to note the size of Aunty's donation.

The next two Sundays, which is all she had, Vyra went again, and I went along with her, even though it got me some funny looks from my pals. Church attendance is about as popular in Shetland as speaking Japanese. There's a small number who do it, but only because they've always done it: their pals treat it like it's an oddball hobby.

Aunty Vyra and Rev. T. MacFadzeon

The Sunday after Vyra and Dracula returned to the Land of Oz, I had a bit of a decision to make: was I going to have the guts to go back to that meeting house without Aunty there to hold my hand, or was I going to forget it and spend Sunday mornings normally, either in the King of Norway or zapping about on the Norton? Actually, it didn't take that long to decide. No way was I going to be born again, or start living like Mr Clean, but I decided to make a regular go of it, well, for a couple of months anyway. It seemed like plain commonsense. People were always saying that Shetland was being transformed by all its modern affluence and not for the better. It was all about Grab nowadays. It just seemed to me that instead of just sitting on the fence moaning about it, at least by going for one little hour a week and listening to a very different take on worldly ways, maybe we could strengthen our own resistance. Yeah, like a 'flu jab maybe. It just seemed like sense to at least hear what the guy had to say. Sure, he didn't have all the answers maybe, but are we so perfect we can afford not to listen?

Soon after, I told the Rev of my momentous decision – just so's he wouldn't think I'd gone all Holy and would shortly be handing him my wallet. "No Way, Dad," I said. Then he talked some himself. He said that folk were not to blame for never going near the churches. It was the churches' fault, that and their unattractive reputation as nests of hypocrites.They had ceased to be relevant. Jesus did not say: "Come unto me and I will bore the pants off you." Nor did He speak in theological gobbledegook like some goddam psychologist. Read the parables, he said. His stories and his language were as simple as could be. Being kicked out of the C. of S., he said, was the best thing that ever happened to him. He saw it as the hand, or Boot, of God. It forced him, if he wanted to continue with his calling, to make his style acceptable and immediate, lively and welcoming, above all really challenging to the normal punter.

"Like me," I said.

"Are you normal?" he queried.

Then I told him I'd be giving up calling him Dad. "Thank you, my son," he said. "I'll be calling you Father from now on," I continued. "Father MacFadzeon. Appropriate, yes?"

He looked heavenward. But he didn't cross himself.

I'd like to say that from this time forth I became a changed man: upright, God fearing, not given to boozing, bad language and horsing around, showing compassion on debtors and maybe even making an honest woman of Nora the Nort Isles Woman. Very few folk can improve themselves permanently without regular help. Try dieting. People going to listen to the Gospel being preached are NOT saying: "Look at me, guys, I'm GOOD!" Absolutely the opposite. They're saying: I'm pretty dodgy and need a bit of help with my life, so I'm going in here to try and get it: why don't you come in too? Trouble with the Church is it has a very bad reputation, so it really does take courage to go there. I mean, in Shetland, would you get a worse name being seen going into a church or into a brothel? Maybe that's why so many Shetland men never go into a church till they're dead. Either that or they think they're perfect.

CHAPTER 11: ERTIE MOVES WI' DA TIMES.

When you see photos of the '70s and '80s nowadays, at least if you lived through those times, they make you feel distinctly queasy. All those tight-arsed flared trousers, frilly shirts, large check jackets with huge lapels, silly shoes, bouffant hair-dos and side-whiskers. And that's just the women. Rightly described by some philosopher as The Era that Style Forgot, it was nevertheless a time when folk were making money in Shetland as never before. The days of the second-hand motor cycle bought out of the Exchange and Mart had vanished forever, to be replaced by the age of the Poncemobile, and especially perhaps the Ford Capri with painted-on flames, big speakers, CB aerial and fluffy dice. Oil men and oil money were everywhere. That most un-Shetlandic of sports, Showin' Deesel' Better aff as dy Neebours, had arrived on the same plane as Tinsel Town.

Ertie now moved with the times. He sold Blessed Assurance to Tommy "Empty Chair" Johnson and didn't do too badly out of it. One of his strategically placed acreages at Gremista he sold for an enormous sum to Grabola Pipes and Drums for a supply base. And on the other bit he built himself a new business: Thrust Motors of Shetland. Ertie knew B-all about motors. He didn't even drive one at that time. All he knew was the new style Shetlander was going to be a sucker for big flashy cars and he, Ertie Spence, that had spent over four years of his life in one of Hitler's stalags with his old chum Big Robbie Voar, living on crusts and jackboots up the bum, was going to make damn sure they got what they wanted from him. The vast showroom was up and running in less than six months, carpetted wall to wall and full of the most desirable, gleaming, glitzy, latest models. When folk went to Lerook, they'd be sure to "Hae a peerie look in at Ertie's, just to see what's doin'," and then they'd go away and find they couldn't stop thinking about it and, not much later usually, they were on the 'phone to discuss terms. There was an office with nice young ladies specially waiting to discuss terms. It really didn't take long: they saw to everything for you. "Dey couldna hae been mair helpfu'," folk often said. Usually, the wee man with the bow tie was there in person to chat with you. Folk liked the personal touch. "I hed a wird wi' Ertie aboot it," they said. So that was all right then.

And of course, no show without Punch. I was in there too, in a sharp suit. Even the "Captain" was resurrected. "I'll just speak to Captain Voar about that," the girls would say when there was any little hitch or anything that needed a bit more muscle to sort out than a sweet smile and a pretty shape. Ertie, for reasons known to himself, had been generous to little me. Well, it was partly on Dad's account I reckon, and partly, I suppose, because he must have been reasonably satisfied with my service to date. I got shares in the new business, was one of the directors in fact, and general manager at the sale room. Not that I knew that much about cars. I'd learned to drive in the Army and always had one since then, but I was never keen on them as I was about old bikes. Anyway, we now employed garage men who were experts – brother Bazz among them – so I didn't need to know it all. Just the latest flim flam from the manufacturers. And of course how to make sure the punters paid up and came back smiling, because to be anyone at all in the new, fun-lovin', Flash Harry Shetland it isn't enough to have a flash car: it has to be a bang-up-to-date flash car, not some rusting heap from two years back. If insurance and loan sharking had been a racket, this was gold mining in very shallow soil.

While all this commercial adjustment was going on, Old Daa handed in his running shorts and headed for the City of Gold and the Harbour Bright. Rev MacFadzeon took his funeral service because he'd been Daa's minister many years back when he was up at the big manse. The folk were so taken with his service that some of them got around to asking the Rev Father if he could set up a branch of the Huttites in Mid Yell, the C of S being as moribund there as in most places. Always on the lookout for more paying customers, he agreed with alacrity, and soon he was taking fortnightly meetings there attended by folk who sensed their lives were missing something that wasn't going to be satisfied by flash cars, bigger and better TVs and even the new bungalows that were sprouting up around those hallowed shores like mushrooms in manure.

Shortly after this, I got together with Chimmie, who now took over Daa's croft, and Chookie, who was up at Ooter Gerdie, and we had a bit of a discussion. Chimmie was still at the Canning Factory but he wanted a job on the rigs or at least at Sullom so's he could rake in more dollars. However, I put it to them that there were other ways besides selling one's body to Grabola. Fish farming for one, and where better than Mid Yell voe? They both liked the idea. Chookie's wee son George was already at Secondary school, and Chimmie's bidie-in Sharon had two young lads from a previous campaign. A fish farm, properly run and financed, could eventually employ them as well, and all of 'em still at home to tend the native soil, instead of shivering on some platform in the North Sea and totally knackered by age 45 – if you got to age 45. So we signed up and I provided most of the money from what I'd been saving working for Ertie, and it all took off from there. It was hard work for Chimmie and Chookie, but unlike the hard work of the past, this stuff paid off. Oh and by the way, they called their new boat after Grandad's old fishing boat: The Laughing Trow.

Not that our lot didn't get their share of the oil jobs. Herkie gave up his Merchant Navy Career to work on the rigs but went back to sea after that. Ruby worked on an accommodation ship in Sullom, and went to Australia after it sailed away. Jessamine was a deckhand on the Narvik Ocean Driller. Laurelina worked on several rigs in the catering line, then went to Aberdeen after that, where she has a good job as a catering manager with Grabola. She's there yet and has a lovely, posh house up Mid Stocket way: she and her man, Samson, who works offshore in the Philippines, are rolling in it. Bozo worked in the pipe yards outside sunny Wick for a while but got done by the coppers for drugs and went to Saudi after that, where he was locked up again. After that he came back to Shetland and lives up at Ladies Drive with his bidie-in Shiraz. Mop was lucky because she'd just left school when Thrust started up and she got an office job there.

CHAPTER 12: SAGA OF SUSIE WONG.

Mind you, sister "Susie Wong" has done best of all oota da oil. She started off on an accommodation rig in the Narvik field, and took off from there with Olaf the Driller, a Norwegian giant from beyond the Arctic Circle. His company, Viking Drillers, were the first to drill on the West side of Svalbard. It was pretty rough there for a while and it got worse when the Danish oil giant, Danskol chartered them to drill off Greenland. Wong went everywhere her man went, and worked with a will: she even had a Safety ship named after her, the SUSIE WONG B. There are various suggestions what the "B" stood for. Then they split up as Olaf took to drink, and Wong settled down with Grit-Vik the Greenlander on the shores of a frozen fiord which thawed out for about six weeks in summer, when Grit would fish for polar bears and Susie would skin them, hack off the blubber to boil up and make oil, which was later shipped out to the USA, for use in the cosmetics industry. They got a good price for it as it was supposed to make women look young again. Talk about an uphill task. In the winter, the whole place closed down and they hibernated.

Then three years later, Olaf the Driller came looking for Wong, who by this time had given birth to three mighty sons. He and Grit-Vik fought with axes, but the Driller won, killed him, chopped him up, roasted him and ate him. Then Grit-Vik's sons, young though they were, called aloud on Thor the Thunderer for vengeance, and their childish cries did not go unheeded. As Olaf was preparing to leave after his meal, with Susie Wong trussed up like a turkey across his broad shoulders, an enormous bear lunged at him out of the howling darkness. But Olaf the Driller, as mighty a man as any Viking between here and Miklagard, threw Susie at the bear, giving him time to draw his axe and hack the monster's blood-dripping head from its huge body. He had reckoned however without Grit-Vik's three sons. While their father's slayer fought the bear they had extracted a massive burning log from the blazing fire, dowsed one end with water so that they could hold it, and when Olaf bent down to pick up Wong out of the snow, they rammed the blazing log… Well, you can guess the rest. If that wasn't a painful end, what is? The little lads could not even be charged with anything criminal as the eldest was only four.

For a while, they left Susie lying there all trussed up with strips of polar bear hide in minus 40 degrees of cold while they debated whether or not they needed her any more. Eventually, after she'd promised to serve them hand and foot and not interfere with any of their childish whims, she was released and spent the next six months cooking for the lads as they gorged themselves on tinned food, packet cakes, pemmican and blubber, becoming in the process more monstrous than human. When the summer came again, Susie got their permission to set off on her snow shoes to get to the trading post fifty miles away on the edge of the fiord, for by then all their food supplies had been used up and the lads were threatening to eat her. While she was away, they intended to raid the settlement they said lay on the other side of the mountain that rose behind their cabin. They took Grit-Vik's gun and axe and Olaf's axe, so they were not going there to sing hymns.

As she waited her turn at the trading post, Susie fell into conversation with a big seaman, Capt. Lars Bars, whose ship, the Narf, was tied up at the jetty. It didn't take her long to persuade the Captain that she was good at cooking, had plenty experience at sea and could make life a lot more cheery for everyone on board, especially himself of course, if given half a chance.. As Lars had been at sea for six months and had only come ashore to buy a ticket for the Danish State Lottery, he found her offer irresistible. That's how Susie got back eventually to Lerwick. She sold her story to the Sun and appeared on several TV shows so she didn't do too badly. Even better when a letter arrived from a Narvik lawyer telling her Olaf the Driller had left her a fortune in his will, provided she wasn't still living with Grit-Vik the Greenlander. As soon as she read this, she nipped outside and chucked a couple of Grit's knucklebones into the bin. She'd kept them as a keepsake, but as she said herself, there's no use living in the past. With the proceeds, she bought herself a posh new house out at Gulberwick, alongside all the nouveaux toffs there, the first of our family in Shetland to live anywhere other than in a croft house or a council house or a shed. She named it "Ma Hoose," but the rest of us called it Wong Kong. The only worry she had was in case any of her three sons turned up there from Greenland. That could be awkward. Not that she was worried for herself, but there probably wouldn't be much left of Gulberwick if the lads took it into their heads to do a bit of pillage and burning on a winter's night.

I rather hesitate to continue the tale of my own humdrum existence after some of this. The spirit of adventure was certainly alive and well in Shetland in those great days.

My spare time activity, colourless and uninspiring by comparison, continued to be old motor bikes. The collection had all been gathered out of old sheds, fallen dykes, rubbish tips and similar uninspiring locations, and brought back to life by my own efforts. None of them was the sort of classic restoration job you can see at shows, not that I have anything against them but it's a different sort of hobby that. Besides the Norton 16H, I had a BSA M20 and a 1937 Triumph 250: all of these had side-valve engines, surely the simplest and most straightforward internal combustion engine ever invented. There were various Francis Barnetts and a James and a DOT: these had Villiers two-stroke petroil engines of various sorts, again a simple straightforward engine to take apart and put together again, ideal for a person with more enthusiasm than technical know-how – i.e. me. Starting them while warm was their only weakness. The 1953 DOT was actually a scrambler, a brilliant little bike in snow, which I'd collected, thanks to the late Colin Inkster, from a hen-house in Gutcher. And there were also various precious machines I never did get going on the road, the oldest of the lot being a 1927 Raleigh horizontally opposed, fore-and-aft twin, with one of the old flat tanks, and wooden foot boards.

The collection had long outgrown Mother's old shed. After a lot of sweet talk and negotiation I persuaded Susie to let me keep them in the big double garage she had at Gulberwick. That was the nearest I ever got to moving among the upper classes.

Susie soon tired of doing housework in her swish new bungalow and gazing out to sea. After obtaining information from me about some of Ertie's commercial properties in town, she made an appointment to see the Cooncillor Himself and, after confirming that, thanks to the late Olaf, she had the readies, she bought the old Excelsior Ladies and Gents Outfitters shop at the corner of King Zog Street and Norrie's Row. An essential part of this bargain was that the Cooncillor would support her subsequent application for a licence to purvey alcoholic liquors, for with Ertie behind it it would almost certainly sail through *nem con*, as the Latinists have it. She reckoned it was a near perfect site, and only a few months later DRILLERS was officially declared open by up-and-coming Country and Western singer Hiram Bluegrass III, whereafter the tinsel grabbers, the trendy with-it set and bemused oil workers who didn't quite know what to do with it all had a glitzy new cabaret bar to support. And support it they certainly did. Hiram gave it a great start, performing some of his best-loved numbers, including D.I.V.O.C.R.E. (specially written for his dyslexic son, George), Stand By Your Flan (for his wife Marylou, an amateur cook), and of course Poor Little Old Wino Me, a true C and W classic. Hiram was just the start. Soon after came Hiawatha the Male Stripper ("This guy had feathers you'd never have believed possible," wrote Shetland Times Culture Correspondent J. Robertson), Sonny and Sher double act Beebee and Nick, Punk band Rock Dobbie and the Abstracts, Sex Pistols tribute band Margaret and Brian, and many, many more. If it was real Shetland culture and a great night out you were after, DRILLERS was definitely for you.

I could hardly keep away from the place, and it was crowded with punters most nights. Who back in 1948, running back and fore to Burravoe on an ancient motor bike to buy a bottle of VP, would have believed Shetland would ever support outfits like this? But the best of it was the profits were going to Sister Susie, not to some sooth company. Behaviour could occasionally cause a few problems as it does in most oil towns, but this was solved once and for all when two of Wong's enormous sons, Ulf and Grit showed up and she immediately gave them jobs as bouncers. Thereafter punters behaved themselves like lambs, no matter how drunk they were: it also kept Ulf and Grit off the peaceful suburban streets of sunny Gulberwick.

The lads had had an eventful time since Susie had left them on her snow shoes. With money they looted from the neighbouring settlement, they managed to reach the States, where they took a course in Bank Heists and Hold-ups at the University of Saint Ignatius Loyola in downtown Baltimore. Here, their tutor, Father Aloysius, had commended their efforts but pointed out that they were hindered somewhat by not being able to read, or speak English. They did well on the practicals. Thus equipped, they soon got jobs as bank robbers with Little Tony's Mob in New Jersey. Not only were they good at dynamiting bank vaults, they were also more or less impossible to arrest, as they could toss cops aside like empty milk cartons. In fact, most police forces kept well clear when they heard the Grit-Vikkers were operating in their area. Tony found after a time, however, that they had to be kept busy or they would create mayhem wherever they happened to be. Once they wrecked his favourite pad, which was stuffed with antique furniture, baroque mirrors and fancy beds, all of which were reduced to matchwood, while the scantily clad "hostesses" he employed had to run for their lives, screaming through the streets of downtown Galveston, much to the appreciation of the largely elderly inhabitants. Eventually, Little Tony shopped the lads to the local police chief in return for some favours in the local coke trade and as a result the lads were surrounded by State Troopers in armoured vehicles and arrested. They got 50 year sentences for various heists, and sent to serve their time in the notorious Tuscaloosa State Penitentiary where the temperature seldom dropped below 100 degrees and prisoners spent long hours out in the blazing sun hoeing vegetables under the benevolent eye of armed guards. Because of their reputation, the lads were kept in reinforced concrete bunkers which could get a bit airless at times, so it looked as if they were destined to stay right there for fifty years. Not that they didn't have buddies outside who might have bribed a guard to take them in some dynamite, but they were all scared of Little Tony. It was, after all, on Tony's behalf that the lads had been booked in.

This all changed when Little Tony himself was machine-gunned at a gay party in downtown Memphis, and Rev Fr. Aloysius – known as Father Al – took over the Mob. The Father remembered the lads from their student days – there had indeed been few students quite like them – and he let the State Governor know that if he didn't want his Penitentiary bombed he should release Ulf, Grit and Woden without delay.

On their release they swore they would never touch another vegetable as long as they lived. Father Al naturally had his own ideas about making an honest living out of crime. The Lord, he said, and His Blessed Mother, never gave a damn one way or the other about bank heists, so as far as he was concerned, it wasn't much of a crime. Which is worse? to rob a bank or to run one? as Brecht asked. More of a crime, he said, was being so rich you had more money than you knew what to do with. The banks were repositories for rich folk, and rich folk, said Jesus, could no more go to Heaven than a camel can pass through the eye of a goddam needle. Therefore, robbing banks and redistributing the proceeds among the less well off (i.e. the Mob and their friends, relations etc) was good for everyone including the rich folk, because they'd be better able to get into Heaven if they ceased being rich.

This meant that Ulf, Grit and Woden were back in business. Trouble was their years in the Pen. had slowed them up a mite, and the first time they blew up a bank vault they brought 24 feet of reinforced concrete down on top of Woden. It took a week to dig him out, and when they eventually found him he looked about as human as a screwed-up wet newspaper. After that, Father Al kept the other two close by him as hit men when required like, for instance, to make people pay up moneys they happened to owe the Mob. They were OK at that, they said, but the one thing they couldn't do now was figure things out for themselves. Woden had been the brains of the outfit. So it went on, then one day Father Al was ordered to Rome to get instructions about some new sin the Holy Father had just thought up. He took Ulf and Grit on either side of him, as Rome, he said, has more hit men and mafiosi than Chicago. On the way there, the plane blew up over the Alantic. Police later reckoned this was due to discontented members of the Mob, who'd lost out since Father Al took over because he refused to deal in narcotics or little children. There was wreckage strewn over a wide area, and holding on to some of it were Ulf and Grit, who eventually paddled their way to Stromness in Orkney, where they wrecked a harbour front hotel, and got local police to put them to Shetland where, they said, their dear old heart-broken Mother was praying they'd survived the explosion. (In fact they'd never given Susie a thought since she'd left to go shopping on her snow shoes.) How did they know she was there? Don't ask me, but since the Oil started, the Mob have had their contacts everywhere. Even in Gulberwick.

These two guys Ulf and Grit, whom I had now met for the first time, were my nephews. I sort of felt some responsibility for them, especially when I considered how useful they could be to anyone who had to

Ulf and Grit with Wong

collect money from reluctant punters. They were huge, ugly, intimidating heavyweights, with TUSCALOOSA STATE PEN, tatooed across their foreheads. They wore sharp suits at all times, and under the jackets, shoulder holsters which local police seemed for some reason reluctant to take off them. They made even the hardest red-necked Shetlander look like Michael Jackson. Susie, however, had learned how to handle them: you didn't want to let them near the drink was Rule One. Rule 2 was: Don't serve them a meal with vegetables on the plate, or the first thing that would happen was the plate and all its contents went through the window, quickly followed by the table and chairs. And Rule 3 was: Keep 'em busy. Even going by the rules, living with them wasn't that easy. "It was like it must have been," said Susie, "i'da aald days, when folk lived in ee end o' da hoose an' da animals i'da idder."

They were so effective as bouncers that, with punters behaving like little angels whenever the lads appeared, they had less and less to keep them occupied and they got bored. So they nicked someone's fancy 4 x 4 and rammed their way into the RBS, where staff, as ever, asked them to fill in forms, provide proof of identity, urine sample, Mother's maiden name and hang around for about thirty minutes while they had a word with the accounts manager. Naturally, this irked the lads – as, indeed, it irks many another. They dynamited the safes and escaped through a hole in the wall with the takings, borrowing another big flash car and heading for Gulberwick.

Give them their due, police were quick off the mark, and I've heard it said they'd already formulated an emergency strategy just in case the lads reverted to type. An armed stand-off resulted, with Ulf and Grit holed up in Ma Hoose, and police calling in emergency reinforcements and two armed helicopters from Inverness. About half of Gulberwick was evacuated, and some nouveaux toffs were really rather upset. This was not what they'd expected when they had opted to move to Gulberwick, and that's just what happens when they allow hoodlums in, they said. The riffraff should be kept on their own estates where they can fight among themselves to their hearts content. Were they going to have to move to Quarff?

Eventually, police let me address the lads through a loud hailer. My effort was met with a fusillade that demolished a police car. Police returned fire and it continued spasmodically thereafter. Plainly, Ma Hoose, which, like almost all modern Shetland houses, was no architectural jewel, was going to be a basket case before long. What was really worrying me was my old bikes in Wong's garage. Anyone with a bank account can buy a modern house, but old bikes – they ain't makin' them no more.

As night fell, the place was stormed by armed police, a detachment of the Royal Highland Fusilliers with fixed bayonets and bagpipes playing, and a platoon of the 1st Dunrossness Boys' Brigade led by their intrepid Captain Ian Jamieson. Many sustained life-threatening injuries, and in the course of the action Ma Hoose went up in flames, though the garage remained intact, Ulf and Grit were taken away in chains, and shortly thereafter were returned to the USA when it was discovered they had US citizenship, as provided by Little Tony. Wong, whose life seemed a bit prone to accidents, got a decent insurance pay-out from Tommy, decided against returning to Gulberwick – she felt she didn't really fit in there – and sold the remains of Ma Hoose as a serviced site to an up-and-coming bureaucrat and his lovely wife and sweet little children. I believe they changed the name to Sea View.

Susie now made herself a bijou flat on the top floor of DRILLERS, which was very convenient for her, but no use for keeping old bikes in, being up two flights of stairs. From time to time I had thought about getting a place for myself. I'd even discussed it with Ertie, and he'd advised me to buy a decent modern house for prices were rising and it'd be a good investment. But somehow I didn't really see the need. A single, solitary person wanting to live in a house all on their ownio seems like a recipe for boredom and worse. I was still living at No 8 Provost Freebie Drive and there were only eight others there more or less permanently, plus three little bairns. Mother wasn't bothered one way or the other, and she was the only one whose opinion really mattered. "I'm past caring." she often said. Very often.

However, the bikes had need of a home even if I didn't. So I got Ertie to find me a Council House, and put the bikes in the front bedroom. Fortunately, Andy Leask and his wife Dolores from two doors down were wanting a transfer to Nederdale to be near their grandchildren. Ertie arranged this in next to no time, leaving No. 4 Provost Freebie Drive vacant for little me.

CHAPTER 13: BONZO DOG'S BIG OFFER.

By 1985 I'd say, the brave new glittering world of Shetland the Oil-Rich Emirate had settled in good ways, with snouts in the trough all round. That included me of course. The old ways had already been consigned to the pages of glossy magazines, and written about as if they were back in the early Middle Ages. D and Cs had gone to the wall like just about every other couthy shop on Commercial Street, and folk – or consumers rather, for they'd ceased being a folk really – flocked daily to grab an ever-changing variety off the shelves of supermarkets. If your house wasn't being continually re-built or at least totally gutted, you were definitely odd, and if your motor wasn't the latest, biggest glitzmobile from Thrust Motors, you'd be just as well having "Failure" tatooed across your forehead. Verily, as Marx himself said, the sight of a capitalist community with its collective snouts in the swill bucket and its asses in the air was enough to turn you to Communism.

Like everyone else, I enjoyed not having to scrape and save to buy things I'd always wanted, enjoyed being able to splash out on goodies without thought for the morrow. Trouble was, I suppose, I was too used to old-fashioned hardship to be completely carefree about it. I didn't really need that many goodies, just like I didn't really need a nice new house. I kept thinking the modern age was a swindle: in return for a lot of junk goodies we didn't need, we were giving away something of unique value: a communal, simple way of life. Or as the Book had it: Esau exchanged his birthright for a mess of pottage.

The reason I know it was 1985 was because that's when I received an unexpected offer of an alternative lifestyle that did not involve growing a ponytail, snorting illegal substances or wearing sandals. It was from an old friend: General "Bonzo Dog" Doodah Banda. Well, I say "General". In fact when I opened it up I found that Bonzo had managed to climb a few rungs further up the ladder since those days. The letter heading read: "From the Office of President For Life Field Marshal Comrade George Mzuzikele Doodah-Banda, Peoples Democratic Republic of Magongo."

"Hi Herbie!" it began. "Remember old Bonzo Dog? I hope you do my friend, because I'm getting in touch with a few old comrades. Since the British left here, there was a bit more trouble from our friends the Marxist Leninists which threatened to knock the wheels off our progress as a newly emerging African nation, so myself and a few chums from the RMR – now the Magongoese Peoples Struggle Revolutionary Forces (MPSRF) – decided to set up a Revolutionary Committee of National Unity, with myself as President and Commander in Chief. Okay, it was a military take-over, but all in a good cause. The first thing we did – after nationalising the banks, of course! – was make peace with the ML comrades, and bring them into the government of national unity, after which we declared ourselves a Peoples Democratic Republic and applied to the Soviet Union for fraternal aid. Of course, they were only too delighted to respond. So in other words we took a sharp turn to the left in order to avoid running straight into the abyss of national bankruptcy and collapse that lay before us. We had to take most of our ML chums into the armed forces, creating in the process a somewhat oversized army. That's why I'm writing to you. What we really need now is decent officers who can train and discipline men and make them into decent soldiers. Pay will be good. Opportunities will be yours for the taking. Conditions will be – well, you know what conditions are like here. The main thing is you'll be making a major contribution to a country that needs all the help it can get. How about it, Herbie?

"PS. I've already contacted Capt Gorbals-Fieldfare."

This script took some believing. I'd long since lost contact with Magongoland, and it wasn't a place the newspapers printed a lot about. I think I'd heard that the Army had taken over some time back, but that was not an unusual occurrence thereabouts. The British had left pukka democratic constitutions, parliaments, etc in their colonies, blissfully forgetting that democracy had taken about four hundred years to develop in Britain, so how were Africans supposed to get it up and running in a few years?

I re-read the letter many times. To begin with, what Bonzo was proposing seemed totally out of the question. I was 45 years old, far too ancient to resume active military service after a long time away from it. There was the climate and the jungle as well. Also, thanks to Ertie, I already had a very decent job, and selling motors in the present economic climate in Shetland was almost a job that did itself. But did I really want to go on doing that for another twenty years? The more I thought about it, the more it tended to look like a preposterous waste of a life. I'd been a lucky lad so far, but only because I'd always taken any opportunity that came along. Here, out of the blue, was another one. A challenge in fact. I was fit, had plenty smackeroolas in the bank, no dependents and was doing a job that was well paid but could in no way be described as a proper challenge for a fit man of my age. So I decided to take up Bonzo Dog's offer without delay. I'd had my snout in the trough. Now I could maybe hold up my head again.

President for Life, Field Marshal George Mzuzikele Doodah-Banda.

CHAPTER 14: MAGONGOGRAD.

Windsor, when I eventually got there, had changed. It had changed its name to Magongograd for a start. But it was still as hot and steamy as ever. There on the runway with his backside against the presidential Zim and surrounded by a bunch of his chums, all decked out in neat tropical uniforms was President for Life Doodah Banda, and when I started down the steps the Presidential Pipe Band started up with "Hey Johnnie Cope", a long-time favourite of Magongoese military bands since the original takeover from the French by an intrepid Scotsman, during the Napoleonic war period. It really was a memorable welcome. Sorry for mentioning it, I'm sure.

"Very glad to meet you again, Herbie old fellow!" said Bonzo shaking hands vigorously. He introduced his chums, a few of whom I minded from the old days in Jock Force. Everyone was in high good humour. They know how to welcome people in Magongo. Bonzo took me into the back of the limo, and off we zimmed along the five mile pot-holed highway that stretched in the heat from the airport to Magongograd. En route, large plywood triumphal arches spanned the road, with brightly painted portraits of President Mzuzikele – as he was officially known – in full uniform, bedecked with the flags of friendly nations like East Germany, Belarus, Uzbek SSR and North Korea. But they were not the only sign of progress. The whole of Magongograd was almost as built up with high-rise Communist blocks of flats as downtown Prague. The USSR had been making a contribution in more than rhetoric. "They're not Buckingham Palace," said Bonzo, "but they're a lot better than the shanties that preceded them. They've even got piped water, when it works."

Another surprise awaited me on my arrival for there, ensconced in a comfy armchair and with a well-filled glass on a little table by his side, sat Capt – now Col. – "Mad Jock" Gorbals-Fieldfare, looking a shade greyer but certainly no less mad than in his prime. "Herbie, Old Thing!" he bellowed, levering himself from the chair with surprising agility. I'd heard you were selling motors up in the Arctic Circle somewhere."

After he'd retired fron the PANSIES on full Colonel's pay, Mad Jock had beaten retreat to all that was left of the ancient Highland estates of the Gorbals-Fieldfares, a broken down, midge-infested Bed-and-Breakfast establishment at the far end of a long single-track road in the western Highlands. Here he had tried to put things in decent order, booting out the incumbent local slackers and bringing in enterprising Angles, his aim being to up-market into the posh Highland hotel racket, with himself as cheerful mein host and his long-suffering wife, Patience, as chief cook and bottle washer. This unfortunately had not gone down too well with the dear locals and the crumbling mansion was soon torched, reducing it to a tottering shell which had eventually to be totally demolished. With the proceeds, however, they'd built a modest but altogether more convenient bijou home, intending simply to return to the B-and-B trade when, Hallelujah, the Col had received Bonzo Dog's summons to rejoin the Colours forthwith. Pausing only to stuff his kilt, sword and full-dress uniform into a handy kit-bag, Gorbals-Fieldfare had caught the overnight express from Mallaig – he had to share with a lot of fish – and had not ceased travelling till now, when he had arrived just in time for mid-day drinkie-poos at the Presidential Palace.

The next few days saw the arrival of several other expatriates in varying states of antiquity and inebriation: Capt Fergus Freekirk, from Lewis, who had come by sea and paddled all the way up the great grey green greasy Urumguano in an inflatable canoe; Lt Col Rupert Farbelow; Colour Sgt Ewan "Bonkers" MacDuff, and, older than these by quite a few years, Maj Norman de Landings, DSC and Bar.

At the end of their first week, Bonzo held an official banquet to formally welcome the lads into the Staff College he'd set up in the old MT section attached to what had once been the Queen Victoria Barracks. This beano was attended by the bigwigs of Magongograd, their ladies; wives and women, none bigger than Soviet ambassador Viktor Golubchik, who kicked off the evening in traditional Bolshevik style by proposing toasts to eight of the assemblage, ranging from The President to Honoured Guest Workers, i.e. us. The only trouble with this was he lost quite a few of the dignitaries to insobriety right at the kick-off, and naturally, the Life President was not the man to pale by comparison so he in turn proposed ten more toasts immediately afterwards, ranging from His Excellency the Ambassador of the Union of Soviet Socialist Republics, down to Our Dear Comrades from the Era of Imperialist-Colonialist Oppression, i.e. us. Of course, just as no one could afford to be caught out not responding with enthusiasm to any of the Soviet toasts, neither could anyone fail to lift his glass or chuck the stuff under the table when the Comrade President was doing the honours. This meant, as can be calculated by a simple process of addition – simple that is if you're sitting there reading about it at your ain fireside, not so simple for us trying to do basic addition with vast quantities of Soviet vodka swilling around in our noddles – that everyone was completely blotto before hardly any of the many courses had been consumed so that eating became a thoroughly complicated process if it was to be performed with any degree of propriety. It rapidly became, in other words, a bit of a shambles. Not that the toasts were over for the night: Various civic dignitaries and at least three other ambassadors still managed to struggle to their feet – or were hauled upright by their minders – unfold their carefully rehearsed speeches and give tongue, though what they said in the process is beyond my personal recall. Never, however, in the long and distinguished history of Magongograd was a band more gratefully received when it struck up shortly afterwards than the gentlemen of the Presidential ensemble, giving those left in upright positions a chance to finish some of their meal without further alcoholic diversion.

The fun, however, was not yet over. After what seemed like a quick five minutes, an immaculately dressed majordomo pronounced: "Gentlemen! Take your partners please, for the Boston Two-Step!" Now far be it from me to claim racial superiority over my fellows, but having been born and raised in Shetland these words, heard familiarly through a thick alcoholic haze, seemed from long experience in the slippered halls of my youth to summon one, regardless of condition, to arise without delay and take to the floor like a man. This – whilst all around were comrades tumbling over each other – I did, drew myself indeed to my full height and proceeded directly to the end of the festive board, where sat the President's good lady, Madam Majuba, and bowing before her, begged for the inestimable honour of a Boston Two-Step. She was, I believe, quite chuffed, and it did me

Our Colonel ... navigating the Soviet Ambassador's wife around the dance floor..

no harm either with her Lord and Master. There were few, alas, able to join us on the floor, though I am proud to record that our Colonel Gorbals-Fieldfare himself, was also, despite serious impediment, responding to the Call of Duty, for he was even then, with wrapt attention, navigating the Soviet Embassador's wife around the dance floor like a skilful pilot conning a heavy tanker across a tricky anchorage. As he passed Madam Majuba and I, he winked. Not a lot of men in his state can do that.

The six of us were billetted in an accomodation block in the Staff College. We had complete freedom to run the place and the courses as best we could, and as like Bonzo's own training at Sandhurst as we could make it. Col Gorbals-Fieldfare was in charge, answerable directly to Bonzo. Major de Landings was, by reason of his plenitude of years, a bit old and stiff for jungle training so he was i/c Admin, although he insisted on doing his share of parade ground drills, where he was a tough martinet, greatly to Bonzo's liking. Fergus, Bonkers and I were in charge of the jumping about, Bonkers being a trained PE specialist with the physique to prove it, if somewhat stouter now than in his youth. Lt Col Farbelow had an extra reason for being there: he was the son of the late Sir Evelyn Truscott-Farbelow, the Governor who had been ambushed and shot, back in the 'Fifties. He believed his family was destined to serve Magongo. Later, Rupert was my field commander, and a more dedicated officer was never born.

So that was the set-up. It was up to us lot to make a kirk or a mill of it, as they used to say when they still had functioning kirks and mills. We worked hard and I suppose, like all teaching jobs, the observable fact that your efforts are succeeding gives you that extra energy to go on. The heat was a constant negative, a burden that critics who live in temperate zones know nothing about when they say things like: "Why don't these African blighters get a grip?" It sapped your energy on a daily basis, except in the blessed cool season which came for about six weeks following the annual rains. Of course you arranged as much of the daily work as possible in the cooler parts of the day: early morning just after dawn being the best and a really magic time for about half an hour before you started to feel the sun burning through your shirt again. But of course, whilst the locals all took two hours off for a nap in the afternoon, soldiers couldn't do that: they must be ready at any hour of the day or night, nor will their enemies be knocking off for a siesta at a convenient time. So two afternoons a week, two o'clock to four – the hottest part of the day – we'd be out with our lads in running kit to run a five mile course in the heat. It was diabolical, at least to begin with. Tell you one thing though: it didn't take all that long for the beer gut to diminish. Gradually, from being totally nackered as a result, I got to feeling weirdly like I'd felt an awful long time ago: dare one say When I was young? Certainly fit. Fit for anything.

CHAPTER 15: BYE BYE COMRADES.

There was nothing wrong with the Magongo Army that some decent discipline and training couldn't iron out, which is what we were there for. It took us about five years. The difference by then was pretty massive. Men were smart both on and off duty. Morale was high. They believed they could do what it was their duty to do. Africa was overrun with armies, most of 'em little better than uniformed thugs. The Magongo Army was a real Army. Bonzo was chuffed, and we were rewarded and supplied accordingly. On parades such as National Independence Day, he took the salute with his cabinet chums and you didn't have to be particularly perspicacious to see he was just about up in the air watching the serried ranks march past his podium with immaculate precision. The Magongoese under President Mzuzikele had sound reason to be proud.

Then of course, like everything else in Africa, things fell apart. Nothing in this world is permanent, but in Africa things are less permanent than elsewhere. It wasn't Bonzo's fault and it wasn't ours. Something happened a long way away which to most folks at the time seemed totally inconceivable. The USSR collapsed. A lugubrious Comrade Golubchik had to sell off the embassy office equipment and vodka cellar to get enough money to buy air tickets back to Moscow. The arms supplies, the technicians, the building materials, the easy-term loans to purchase Soviet and East European furniture, tools, vehicles, plant and all the rest of it ceased and vanished overnight as if it had never been. Suddenly, Marxist-Leninism was no longer the shape of things to come: it had no future at all. Who was going to pay for the Army? And what about our salaries?

"The Army, Gentlemen," said Bonzo as soon as he entered the emergency meeting convened in the Staff College maximum security block, "is going to have to fight for a living." He had, he said as he reached for a leather case handed him by an aide, a contingency plan. We would invade Upswapo. First he would give us a little background report.

"When the Belgians left the Congo in a shambles, they attempted to hold onto their Upswapo enclave. This had resulted in immediate uprisings, followed by invasion by the Congo's fledgling – and incompetent – national army, designed to seize control, and amalgamate the enclave with the Congo. Mayhem resulted. In an attempt to restore law and order, the two main diamond companies – United Diamonds (UD) and the French Compagnie des Mines Africaines (CMA) – set up a mercenary army, the Upswapo Defence Force (UDF), and a government under a former civil servant, President Patrick Chinugu. This lot managed to restore some semblance of law and order but did not meet with the approval of the Soviet Union. In their eyes, the government of President Chinugu was really a capitalist puppet regime whose sole *raison d'être* was the continuing exploitation of the natives in the interests of Western diamond merchants. So they sent in Cuban troops from Angola to overthrow the Chinuguist government and establish a Marxist-Leninist state. The result of all this activity can be easily guessed: more mayhem. And so it has gone on to the present day, Gentlemen, although the capital, Rumbaba, though badly mauled, has been held throughout by the UDF. Apart from that, the rest of the territory is little better than a battlefield. Now however, the Cubans, we hope, should be on their way out, since their Soviet paymasters are not paying anyone any more. Our time, Gentlemen, has thus arrived.

"Our contingency plan is not something we have come up with in a hurry, in response to the disappearance of the USSR. It has, on the contrary, been on the cards and discussed by my cabinet colleagues and I over a number of years. In fact it goes back to British times because it was first pointed out by them that ethnically, the tribes of Western Magongo, chiefly the Anugu, and those of the Upswapo enclave are one and the same. In other words, Gentlemen, Magongo has an ethnic claim to Upswapo which we have long pondered. Only now, we are moving our claim into the present.

"The disappearance of the Soviet Union from Africa will cause poor countries to get poorer. Magongo will not be one of these. We are going to invade and conquer Upswapo, get our hands on those diamond mines and make sure that, while no legitimate interests are denied, the benefits are spread as evenly as possible among our fellow countrymen. We will start tomorrow."

CHAPTER 16: INVASION.

The Magongoese Peoples Air Force took to the skies: two Soviet troop carriers, 4 Soviet fighters, 3 Soviet bombers and 2 Soviet helicopters. "Might as well use 'em while they're still in working order," said Bonzo. They circled round Rumbaba dropping leaflets, then landed without opposition on the airfield. I have one of the leaflets here right now. It says, in three languages including English: "Comrades of Rumbaba and Upswapo! The President and People of Magongo have long watched your sufferings with feelings of Brotherly Anguish! For are not your people, the Anugu, also our people? Now we have come to liberate you from all your many oppressors! And unite you forever with the Greater Magongo Republic! Anugu Brothers! People of Rumbaba! Do not resist our Freedom Loving All-Conquering Forces! Welcome them with Open Arms! Join with us for a future of Prosperity and Peace! All property is safe and the Rights of all are personally guaranteed by our Beloved President, Field Marshal George Mzuzikele Doodah-Banda. Long Live the Peoples Democratic Republic of Magongo!"

By the time we got into Rumbaba along the Barking-Thrush Intercontinental Highway, the troops already landed at the airfield had succeeded in securing key buildings on the outskirts of town including the Radio Station and the public toilets, all without a shot being fired. However, they had halted as planned to await the arrival of the bulk of our forces before we moved on the fortified government buildings in the centre of town. These and the UD and CMA headquarters were all of them held by the UDF. Bonzo moved our Soviet tanks through the town. The place was a shambles from previous attempted coups. The big Intercontinental Splendide Hotel, where Jock Force had spent a few memorable nights was a gutted wreck, its remaining walls pockmarked with bullet holes and shattered by explosions. There were bomb sites all over the place. Yet with typical Upswapan nonchalance, business seemed to be going on as usual around us as we lumbered along. There didn't seem to be any welcoming crowds or maidens throwing rose petals. On the other hand, they weren't chucking Molotov cocktails either. In fact, the way everything seemed like continuing as usual, it looked as if the good citizens of Rumbaba had seen it all before.

By mid-day, the central government and commercial area, heavily fortified with concrete blockhouses, was surrounded by our tanks. Bonzo and one or two comrades jumped down. He summoned the Staff College team to accompany him. At intervals along the roadsides were notices: STOP AT CHECKPOINT AHEAD. The final thirty metres or so had been totally cleared of old buildings, giving whoever held the blockhouses a clear field of fire all around. We arrived at the vehicle check point without any shots fired. "Halt!" ordered the sentry. "State your name and state your purpose." "I am President Mzuzikele of Magongo," said Bonzo. "My purpose is to give the defunct regime here a chance to hand over power peacefully. All lives and all property will be respected." The sentry did a smart about turn, and stomped off across the courtyard extending from the checkpoint to the first of the government blockhouses.The concrete was about fifteen feet thick. You could see how they'd managed to hold out here while rival guerrilla groups had robbed, burned, pillaged and blundered around them.

The longer we stopped there in the heat of the sun, the more it appeared clear that whilst our progress thus far had been without hold-ups, final victory was not necessarily a foregone conclusion. These guys, though few in number, had been holding out here one way or another since the early 'Sixties, and seen off all attempts to take over the capital.

A cease-fire was declared during which further talks would be held to decide the future of the enclave. Our tanks remained where they were and our troops patrolled the rest of town. Meanwhile, contingents of our forces spread out across the country to take over administrative and military centres, of which there were about six all told. Hardly surprisingly this did not go entirely without incident. Approaching the northern frontier town of Gwelo, situated on a bend in the mighty river Urumguano, a detachment under Rupert Farbelow came under heavy fire from Cuban troops who seemed to be holed up there with no intention of shifting. Fighting was fierce and Rupert's attempt to radio for helicopter support received no reply. Eventually, they stormed the town in a night attack, but there were heavy casualties and the Cubans retained a northern hillside district, where they re-fortified their position by blowing up and bulldozing all the buildings in that sector.

Meanwhile back at Rumbaba, the talks were achieving little. Mild-mannered President Chinugu and his advisers knew how to procrastinate. The advisers included two beefy Americans, Stubs and Burt, the local bosses at United Diamonds, and a very superior Frenchman, M. Maurice Couve de Joinville, a senior executive with the Compagnie des Mines Africaines. In the background but never on the negotiating table, one was aware of the UDF, the mercenary force that had made the Chinuguist stand possible. Their CO, known as Ludo, a lethal type by all accounts, was an Englishman who had started life at Harrow, gone into the Queen's Own Hanoverian Guards as an officer, then blotted his copybook in a fairly spectacular manner, and taken himself off to Africa to go to seed. Having run out of cash fairly quickly at that, he had enlisted as a mercenary with the UDF, soldiering being the only trade he knew, whereafter he had risen through the ranks in the way Englishmen abroad have often done. There was absolutely no doubt he was good at his job. There was no doubt either that whilst we shillied and shallied at the negotiating table, Ludo and his chums were preparing for all eventualities.

Meanwhile the European and US media had splashed the invasion all over the papers and TV screens like it was World War III. There was talk of UN intervention, if things weren't settled amicably, and a rumour that the French, who had garrisons in Gabon, might send helicopter support to the Chinuguists if fighting broke out.

Bonzo issued an ultimatum: Accept his generous terms for incorporation into the Greater Magongoese Republic within seven days, or they would take over by force and without conditions. He ought probably to have given 'em one day not seven, but that's just my opinion. Seven days allowed all sorts of external bodies and interests to become enmeshed in the process.

It also allowed the UDF to open up early on the morning of Day 3 with a great many anti-tank guns we didn't know they had.

CHAPTER 17: THE UPSWAPO WAR.

By then however, I wasn't around. I'd been sent north with a support group to beef up Col Farbelow's continuing stand-off with the Cubans.

These Cubans in Gwelo were tough cookies, and had been in Africa since the Angolan Civil War. They weren't supposed to be in Gwelo but safely back home in their sunny Bolshevik island homeland, being thanked and decorated by Fidel. No one knew why they were there. By the time I got there they were dug in over a hillside position at the north edge of town, and pinning down Rupert's force pretty effectively. They also appeared to have control of a considerable hinterland of jungle and, worst of all, as Rupert told it, they were being supplied through the jungle from a totally unknown source. This meant that they weren't going to run out of ammo. Various attempts by Rupert's force to find and cut this supply route had only resulted in our men being butchered. For this reason, Rupert, who was in spasmodic radio contact with HQ Rumbaba had tried again for helicopter support. They could have located the Cubans' supply line and given it a plastering, but none were forthcoming.

It was over this radio that we first got news of the UDF breakout there in Rumbaba. It couldn't have come at a worse time as far as our little operation was concerned, for we'd just launched a determined united attack on the Cuban position and had in fact succeeded in taking part of their front line defences, mainly bulldozed or bombed-out buildings, many of which we had had to take one by one in fierce hand-to-hand combat.The trouble was that over the crackling radio came orders for Rupert to return at once to base and bring his troops with him. Whether this meant including me and my relief force or not, Rupert took the decision, to leave us at Gwelo with the task of holding on to what we'd already taken, and hoping that the Cubans wouldn't notice that our force had been reduced by four fifths. "Think you can do it, Herbie?" asked Rupert, a good example of a question expecting the answer Yes. "We'll give it a try, Sir," I replied. This after all is what we'd spent five years training for. "Sound fellow!" said Rupert, disappearing rapidly into the jungle with the remains of Rupert Force. "It's up to us now, Lads," I said to my meagre unit. They didn't look all that pleased, but then soldiers never do.

Trouble was, where we'd got to among the rubble of north Gwelo

"It's up to us now, Lads!"

wasn't anyone's idea of a decent front line position: there was no field of fire and behind every shattered wall could be lurking enemy snipers. But on the other hand, to pull back out of there would give a clear signal to the opposition that we were drawing in our horns.

It was probably a daft thing to do, but I decided that the only thing in the circumstances was to press forward with the attack. That way it was just possible, fighting among all these ruins, that our enemy wouldn't realise we weren't quite up to strength. Besides, we did have a few advantages: Rupert had left us forty boxes of grenades and, even better, a supply of Soviet self-firing surface to surface missiles. We opened up with these, noting how the Cuban positions erupted in diabolical smoke and flames. Then we charged forward with fixed bayonets, chucking grenades and spraying automatic fire as we went, slaughtering every living thing we came across. There wasn't a man among us who didn't know with exceptional clarity that it was either them or us. Pussyfooting about was definitely out.

It took us about two terrible hours to clear the place entirely, one of the most exhausting two hours of my life, but also – let's not beat about the bush, chums, – one of the most successful. We had won a notable victory and against all the odds. There were a few of them left alive who ran for their lives into the jungle. We didn't follow: frankly we were too utterly amazed that we'd done it, we really couldn't get our heads around any more. The rest were dead and we were alive, and jubilation was the general idea. The Cubans themselves took no prisoners and neither in this instance did we: in our case we simply couldn't afford to. There were too few of us. Besides, they knew the surrounding jungle a lot better than we did. We reckoned they wouldn't be back in a hurry, and in the event we were right.

There followed a night of celebrations in bombed-out Gwelo. But the next little problem was: how were we going to keep control of a town of some 40,000 inhabitants with a force of less than 120 men? The only answer was, in a word, Discipline: the same answer to most of life's little problems. Fortunately, there were people in Gwelo who rapidly concluded they'd probably be better off under us than under the Cubans, and who came forward – with a little friendly persuasion – and volunteered their help in getting the place up and running again. The likely ones among them we trained for a police force to help us restore law and order. The rules they had to enforce were simple: do what you're told or get shot. It's always best to keep things simple. People caught on quick. Within four weeks it was safe for anyone, man, woman or child, to walk the streets of Gwelo: at any time, day or night. I'm sure some people reading this are going to say: What a fascist! Call it what you like: it worked. And by then, we were beginning to learn what had been happening back at the ranch.

CHAPTER 18 : STUBS AND BURT BITE THE DUST.

The UDF break-out had been a major success for the Chinuguists: it certainly took Bonzo and Co. by surprise. Not only was it well planned, it was co-ordinated with useful support from unmarked helicopter gunships that appeared from nowhere and started shooting the hell out of our guys just as the UDF had succeeded in knocking out fourteen of our tanks. It was a major setback for our lads: total shambles in fact, but that's when the discipline kicked in. We were badly mangled but we did not run for the bushes. Capt Freekirk and his little group brought down two of the helicopters with surface to air missiles – later we were able to confirm they were French and had come across from Gabon in cahoots with M. de Joinville. Our own planes were in the air, shooting down the other helicopters and bombing the government fortress, whilst such of our tanks as were still in action bombarded the concrete. Ludo and Co dodged through the town, creating more mayhem and making lightning attacks on our troops from the rear to cause maximum casualties before disappearing back into the labyrinth of narrow streets. They knew the place in detail, including the Queen of Heaven, which they now blew up, after clearing out the workforce beforehand – a rare example of compassion on Ludo's part – and used it thereafter as a supply base. Mad Jock detailed Bonkers MacDuff to run Ludo and Co to earth and eliminate them, but Bonkers failed to get close enough. Ludo was a man of infinite resource.

This roughly was the state of play over a period of three days during which the Chinuguist HQ took a battering but did not fall down whilst Ludo succeeded in destroying several of our planes on the ground at the airport, which he also seriously damaged with explosive devices, though he didn't succeed in putting it totally out of use.

Late in the evening of the third day of this, Bonzo received a secret visit under flag of truce from Stubs and Burt. They told him they were prepared to dump President Chinugu, call off their mercenaries and agree to Upswapo becoming part of Magongo provided Bonzo would guarantee that United Diamonds would be able to continue to own and run their own mines. It would be up to de Joinville, they said, to make his own agreement. But Bonzo was having none of it. His original terms, he said angrily, had promised them exactly what they were now asking for. They'd had their chance, and instead they'd caused a very bloody and unnecessary conflict which would continue now, he said, till he, President Mzuzikele, received the Chinuguist régime's unconditional surrender. Thereafter, all diamond mines in Greater Magongo would be nationalised. The Americans, he said with considerable force, had been exploiting Magongo's wealth for many years: they'd had their share and more than their share. Now the remaining wealth would be fairly exploited for the benefit of all the natives. The only thing he would offer them now, he said, in exchange for immediate surrender, was that the UD and CMA management could

Bonzo Dog talks with Stubs + Burt.

continue to run the mines, to be paid in accordance with a contract that would make allowances for increased productivity and good practice. They asked for a twelve hours truce to discuss it with their people in the US, but this Bonzo also refused. They could discuss it while they were fighting; as they'd started it in the first place. Gorbals-fieldfare, who was present throughout this little exchange said the Americans were lucky to get out of there alive, for all the mayhem, death and misery of these last few days had been caused, in Bonzo's opinion, by the greed of these two men. They were war criminals, in his opinion, and not only war criminals but traitors, because they were prepared to sell their own leader, President Chinugu, down the river in exchange for diamonds. Had they been captured and taken prisoner, Bonzo would certainly have had them shot, but in the event, he didn't get that opportunity.

Whether or not Stubs and Burt ever did get to converse with their US chums it didn't do them much good. The Chinuguists were even madder at them than Bonzo when they found out their American buddies had been trying to two-time them. Unfortunately for Stubs and Burt they'd allowed Ludo to go off with almost the whole of his men, leaving behind insufficient to serve as bodyguards in time of need and if things turned nasty. Things now did turn nasty. Mild-mannered president Chinugu might have appeared a glove puppet of the UD and CMA, but he did have native supporters and they now turned on Stubs and Burt and massacred them. Apart from the personal inconvenience this caused Stubs and Burt, the trouble with this was that Ludo and his mercenaries were on the UD payroll: without Stubs and Burt to sign the cheques, their role in the present conflict was at an end. Accordingly, they left off attacking the Magongoese Army and airforce, and robbed the National Bank of Upswapo instead, before disappearing down the road to the DRC in their own army lorries. The Chinuguists were on their own.

News travels fast and far nowadays, sometimes too fast for its own good. It can be transmitted all round the world before it's been checked for accuracy. That's what happened now. Some scoop-happy reporter in down-town Rumbaba sent off a shock-horror about how Stubs and Burt had been brutally massacred by Bonzo and Co. The Life President had already acquired something of the status of a Croatian war criminal in the Western Media. This did not improve his image.

CHAPTER 19: A SAILOR'S FAREWELL.

The disappearance of Ludo's little army with the contents of the National Bank finally convinced President Chinugu that it was time to come to terms with Bonzo. Upswapo, after all, had been a shambles for nearly thirty years, frequently looted and shot up by jungle warlords. If rule from Magongograd – soon to revert to Windsor – was going to mean peace and security, it was definitely time to find out more. So the fighting stopped. Impromptu celebrations started, citizens dancing in the battered streets with Bonzo's soldiers. They were, after all, brothers not foreign oppressors. Bonzo and President Chinugu greeted each other like Esau and Jacob and settled down in civilised fashion to discuss what could and should be done. It really did begin to look as if, at last, Upswapo's post-colonial future might be of benefit to the natives and not just to diamond merchants and their share-holders.

Then the unexpected happened. Bonzo received an E-mail from the USS Ticonderoga which, it said, just happened to be anchored three miles off the coast of Magongo and directly opposite Magongograd. The message was short and to the point. It read: Get your goddam army out of Upswapo by 5pm Tuesday or we bombard your capital. Signed: Rear-Admiral Curtis le Strange, USN.

"Dammit," said Bonzo. So far, he and his little helpers had, between them, thought of everything. But not this. Obviously, the demise of the Soviet Union had left the US free and happy to exercise a bit of muscle in African waters without the worry that Moscow might nuke the White House. The liberty of small nations with diamond mines owned by large US companies had to be safeguarded, and nasty military dictators who killed rich Americans had to be slapped down. That's what the Rear Admiral was there to do. Soon, a large, bulky plane came droning overhead, landing carefully on the one useable runway at Rumbaba International Airport. The back fell open and out rolled a Humvee, some smaller vehicles and about fifty US Marines. They left a heavy guard on the plane to make certain none of the natives got their cute little fingers on it, then the rest roared off down the pot-holed road to Rumbaba, a US flag flying from the bonnet.

Rear-Admiral le Strange was a large, imperturbable East coast Yankee. He was a little perturbed, when he found the two sides, rather than hammering each other's forces, as he expected were in fact engaged in fraternal conversations and occasional games of football (a game the Rear Admiral frankly didn't understand anyway). He was a little more perturbed when he discovered that Stubs and Burt had not been chopped up by the bad guys, but by the good guys he had come to rescue. And he was perhaps a little more perturbed when Bonzo introduced him to Col Gorbals-Fieldfare, a charming if somewhat elderly British officer who appeared to have a senior position in the invasion force. Then there was mild-mannered Patrick Chinugu. He listened politely to offers of generous US aid, then told Curtis not to bother. No amount of US aid, he said, would make Upswapo a viable, independent state: it would merely keep it subservient to foreign control and a sitting target for all the envious neighbours. If anyone knew, he did, he said. Politely. He had come to the conclusion that it was in the best interests of the people of Upswapo to amalgamate with their Magongoese brothers. They could defend the country, and he believed President Mzuzikele was honest enough to exploit the diamonds for the good of all. Diamonds were no use to Upswapo if, as had been the case for thirty years, they were too weak to protect their own people. That, he said, was all he wished to say.

The Rear-Admiral was a bit perturbed by all this. The situation was plainly not as he had been briefed by the Pentagon. Some face-saving was plainly in order. "At the very least, Mr President," he said, "Washington will expect a properly conducted referendum, giving every Upswapan citizen, male and female, the opportunity to vote For or Against the union."

President Chinugu demurred. Bonzo demurred. President Chinugu gave some cogent reasons why this proposal was a waste of time and counter-productive. But President Chinugu was well used to humouring powerful white men, especially Americans. If he had to hold a referendum to get the Rear-Admiral off his back then that's just what he would do. Admiral le Strange heaved a sigh of relief. He had saved face. He shook President Chinugu's hand energetically. He gave Bonzo a wintry smile. Then he got into his Humvee and they all headed back to the airport. President Chinugu and Bonzo followed behind to see them off. It didn't take them long to load up. The mighty engines roared, the big plane taxied slowly forward until it ran over one of Ludo's explosive devices and disappeared forever in a truly cataclysmic detonation. Bonzo and President Chinugu dived for cover as the bits started returning to earth.

Bonzo + President Chinnsu see off the Admiral.

"Reckon we can forget about that referendum, Patrick old chep," said Bonzo.

All these alarums and excursions amounted to one thing in the end: Victory! Bonzo's army had proven itself capable of winning a real war, and the Life President Field Marshal was totally unstinting in his praise both for his men and for us old sweats who, he said, had knocked the blighters into shape in the first place. There was, of course, a massive Victory Parade through the jubilant streets of Magongograd, now again renamed Windsor as Marxism-Leninism had plainly had its day. I am proud to say I was there to take part and, along with many others, to receive my specially minted Magongo Diamond Star medal. Rupert Farbelow had been more than generous in his report to Bonzo about how "Capt H. Voar and his assault group, left to their own slender devices at Gwelo by the vicissitudes of war, had driven out a much larger Cuban occupying force and had thereafter taken over the running and defence of the aforesaid frontier town, restored law and order, organised basic rebuilding and public services, and in fact provided a more effective administration there than had existed at any time in living memory."

"Seems you've got talents as an administrator we knew nothing about, Herbie, Man!" said Bonzo, pinning the Star on my manly chest and shaking hands warmly.

"First I knew about them," I said.

"Tell you what," said the Life President, always a quick thinker, "How d'you like to continue out there as Governor? We'll be appointing Governors to the six towns in Upswapo, and Gwelo is a key location. It's going to need a military man anyway, and there'll have to be a small garrison. You could keep the cheps who've been serving with you if you like, and pretty much a free hand otherwise. What say, Herbie, ma Man?"

I was totally thrilled. For the lad from Provost Freebie Drive, becoming a provincial governor seemed a bit of an achievement. I took one step back. Crashed down my foot as I snapped to attention. Saluted. "Sah!" I said.

This was better than loan sharking in Lerook.

CHAPTER 20: GOVERNOR OF GWELO.

Heaven forbid that I should give the impression that it was only little me who did anything noteworthy in the Upswapo war. Major Norman de Landings had successfully defended the Water Tower against prolonged UDF assault. Bonkers MacDuff, as previously noted, after giving Ludo and Co a run-around in the alleyways of downtown Rumbaba and holding out till nearly the very end in the Queen of Heaven Nite Club Bar, had with four of his men disguised themselves as Nite Club ladies and infiltrated Chinuguist HQ, where they slit the throats of two colonels, a major-general and a Belgian mining engineer who'd all thought they were in for a good time. Thereafter, Bonkers and Co had shimmied into the HQ canteen, where they had pies and chips and a few pints before blowing it all up on the way out. Col Farbelow, besides launching the attack on the Cubans at Gwelo, later took over command of the 2nd Battalion MPSRF – now reverting to its old name The Royal Magongoese Rifles – when its own Colonel was killed in action. He led the assault on the rear of the government compound and was in process of occupying the anti-tank battery when the cease-fire was called. Col "Mad Jock" Gorbals-Fieldfare served throughout as personal aide to FM Doodah-Banda, giving him timely and appropriate advice at all times both when called for and frequently when not called for. Bonzo described his contribution as "indispensible." Besides being permanently attached to Bonzo's staff, Gorbals-Fieldfare also managed to sneak out one night disguised as a bucket man. He gained entry to the CMA block house through the latrine shaft, waited for M. Couve de Joinville to enter the convenience to unburden himself, then removed his head. Next morning, his servant found him still sitting there, minus his head, which Jock presented to Bonzo later that morning. It was entirely due to

His servant found him next morning

Bonzo's categorically forbidding the Colonel from doing the same next night to Patrick Chinugu that the Upswapan President survived the war. This initiative of Mad Jock's explains why we have not heard much about the superior Frenchman during the foregoing pages.

So I returned to Gwelo as Military Governor. Fourteen years of hard but rewarding work followed, by no means all of it mine. Security was the first – and continuing – concern for we were within five miles of the DRC frontier across which lurked mayhem on an institutionalised scale, the jungles being infested with bandits and murderous thugs, some of 'em politically inspired, many just wandering tribesmen like the Rugs, whose traditional ways had been disrupted by all the fighting. Gwelo was traditionally a trading town, positioned on a bend in the great grey green greasy Urumguano, but its trade had sadly diminished. Now, with the establishment of a stable government, we hoped to revive it. To do this we had to keep the baddies out.

I started by acquiring as much heavy earth-moving equipment as I could beg, buy, borrow or steal, then set the population to work constructing a massive wall all around the town, with fortified towers at strategic points along it and concrete fortified gateways at our four entrances. Yes, it was probably thanks to my dear old history teacher, Aggie Bell, who all those years ago had told us in gripping style about Hadrian's and Antonine's efforts in North Britain to keep out the heathen Caledonians and Picts. I told you she was a good teacher. If mad. I'd even, since then, read a bit somewhere about the truly massive fortifications built by the later Roman Emperor Theodosius II around his capital, Constantinople, to keep out the barbarians in the fifth century – walls that were never successfully breached for a thousand years, and only then after cannon were used on them by the Turks in 1453. Herbie's Wall wasn't quite in that league, but it was built to keep out marauding bands just like Hadrian's, and as such it worked. Not just that, but by engaging everyone's capacities, although there was plenty moaning about "slave labour" to begin with, the big effort with the very visible result had the happy effect of raising the population's morale. Folk began to feel they were all working together for the common good. Back to the Dark Ages I suppose. Any vehicle coming into town had to stop at one of the gateways for checking: it was not possible any more to drive straight in. Armed troops controlled the gates. Again, there were complaints to begin with, but people soon adjusted: the gates were for the good of all, not to profit some privileged minority.

Major rebuilding of the northern quarter devastated by the fighting also went on apace. We built a big barracks there whilst we were about it. By the way, talking about Hadrian's Wall, I mind Aggie telling us the reason why in the end the Wall was useless was not because of design or building faults, but because they no longer had the manpower needed to man it. By the last years of the Roman Empire, soldiers were in desperately short supply, and naturally the hard-pressed military authorities took troops away from peripheral areas like Britain to beef up defence nearer home. Hence, in the end, the Picts and Caledonians just walked through, NAE BORRA, as the rude Caledonians have it. We didn't have that problem, partly because it was a smaller, more compact area, partly because in Gwelo every fit man and woman had to do what I and my elderly contemporaries had had to do many years ago: National Service. That gave us the manpower to make our fortifications effective and it didn't cost us an arm and a leg either. You had to do it and it was for everyone's good. Actually it was not unpopular and, again, it gave folk a sense of common purpose. Everyone had long ago had enough of the alternative. It also allowed us, over the years, to recruit the best young guys for our permanent army, not that there was ever any lack of recruits. Pay was low, but you got your meals, uniform and somewhere safe to get your head down. If you have lived as the citizens of Gwelo had been living, these are very valuable advantages indeed. The Gwelo Regiment was and remained a crack team.

I would not like it to be understood that everything was run in my time there as part of the military. There were many other aspects and all of them equally challenging, including aspects one might not in the first instance really want to be challenged about, like sewers and sewage. Ignore them at your peril! In fact, a place with a rubbish sewage disposal system is not going to be the best it could be and everyone who lives there knows it. And smells it. People stop trying hard if you expect 'em to live in shit. The Romans knew it, and this is even truer in Africa, where the heat and flies can be overpowering, than in some Norwegian fiord where in any case the answer's pretty obvious. In fact, the answer was obvious enough in Gwelo too and for the same reason: get it all running smoothly into the Urumguano.

So no, it wasn't all military, but defence is an aspect of town and country planning a Governor ignores at his peril. Look at Shetland. They've let in all the riffraff, rich and poor, without a thought on how best to defend their own ways, and now the place is neither one thing nor another: a brash, crossbreed with neither roots nor quality. Of course, yes, it's always been that way there: the same happened during the great herring fishing days. They'll moan about things not being whit dey wir, but they'll never get aff the fence and DO something. Compare the Irish who, when they finally got pissed off with their own dear English master race, drove 'em out and set up their own bloody country. Takes guts. And probably a decent religion as well, something the Shetland Islands have never had since the C of S came in in the sixteenth century to grab their bit of the action.

Apart from defence then – and sewage – two aspects of local government that certainly engaged my attention were health care and education. There had been a dispensary in Gwelo before, established originally by the Belgians, though seldom properly stocked or staffed. The Belgians in fact had been among the worst type of colonial exploiters. Their Congo colony had been a police state, and a mighty brutal one at that, wholly dedicated to exploiting the resources, not at all to improving the very humble condition of the native inhabitants. However, Catholic priests of one shade or another had served at times as doctors. They also trained up nurses, some of whom – as everywhere in the world – became skilled dedicated medics and worth their weight in diamonds. But the priests had fled when they heard that the Bolsheviks were in town, and anyway, there's a worldwide shortage of priests. In my time there, we built a completely new hospital: staffing was the difficulty, but we kept on and on at the multiplicity of international agencies set up to provide medicare in backward lands, and eventually we got our doctors. I also got a very decent Matron, by calling in at the King George V Hospital in Windsor on one of my infrequent trips to town, and begging Maisie Manson from Mossbank – who, as previously mentioned, was a nurse there – to venture up country and take charge. It was no easy option for her, as Gwelo was a remote and fairly primitive place compared to the not inaccessible delights of the capital, and of course it had only recently been the scene of battles. But, like the gold brick she was, Maisie rose to the challenge and decided to become our first ever proper Matron, with all the responsibilities and extra work. I need not add that it was a great boon for me as well, having someone to chat to about the latest world-shattering events in the archipelago – not that Matron Manson had much time to chat! I will add that I now completed the set by collecting Geordie

Halcrow from the ruins of the Jesus Saves Mission on the outskirts of Rumbaba and setting him up with a job teaching English in our new High School. His boss, Rev Mbeki, had been among the casualties in the late internecine strife, and the Mission was in a dire state. I think Geordie considered his new job a blessing though he later opened up a new Jesus Saves Mission in Gwelo, and I was glad to help. I'm sure I need not add that on the all-too few occasions the three of us got together for a few jars, all our multifarious day-to-day concerns vanished like gunsmoke into the tropical night as we yapped and yarned away by the hiss of Tilley lamps in the unintelligible tribal patois of Ultima Thule.

Talking of the High School, education provision in Gwelo was one of my responsibilities. I hadn't been all that keen on education at the dear old Commercial, and left at the earliest opportunity, but, fortunately, few of us retain our early attitudes to education into later life, and many's the time folk can be heard saying: "I wish I'd stuck in better at the school when I had the chance." It was the Army that showed me what opportunities could be got by getting down to it and actually putting stuff into that hard, ba'-shaped object atop your neck, an object many folk just leave empty or, worse, stuff with useless and often poisonous junk. My brush with Tom "Feeble" Ferris, sometime knitting maestro and Director of Education Sport, Dog Racing and Family Planning, had awakened me to the miserable dumbing down of modern education. It had shocked me then and continued to do so. Scotland after all has always been a poor country. Only two things invited the admiration of outsiders: its first rate education system open to all regardless of wealth or class, and its banks. The banks, after over three hundred years of pawky profitability are now on the trash heap due to a corrupt combination of greed and folly that no traditionally run Scottish bank would ever have permitted. Education has gone the same way, and for the same reason: traditional, commonsense values have been dumped and crack-brained, mediocre theories given free rein. The one class of folk who previously benefitted most from traditional Scottish education – the ordinary working class – have suffered most from the result, because middle class or well-off parents still have the money to ensure their progeny can be educated to best effect: all that's on offer for the majority is fifth rate entertainment, leading to vacuous college courses for thickos to keep 'em off the streets.

In Gwelo we wanted and got traditional schools, and Bonzo was 100% in favour. In fact he applied the same standard across the country.

Magongo needed the same standards as had once helped make Britain into an Empire. Prize giving days and Sports days were big events in Gwelo schools. Maybe in a degenerate country like the UK, prizes or placing pupils in order of merit are harmful – so they say – but in a country with its way to make in the world, inculcating a desire to strive, a determination to succeed and to finish the course, a dogged perseverance to achieve – these are the virtues a proper school system encourages, in my opinion. Teachers need to be keen, well educated and a decent example, not mental or moral slackers. A Headmaster needs to be hard working, but above all a natural leader for his pupils, a source of discipline and encouragement, respected but also liked, at times jovial. If someone lacks these necessary talents to teach or to lead, no amount of advice or college courses will make a decent teacher out of him or her.

Having said all of which, Education has beggared many African states by creating a class of young men and women who think they're too clever to till the soil or follow traditional ways. Unable to get the sort of jobs they think their learning entitles them to, they sit around all day criticising the government and their elders, making trouble and providing fertile soil for malcontents and revolutionary bampots. In Magongo we countered this modern plague by National Service. Our youth were no sooner stuffed full of half-baked reforming fervour than they were whisked off to march up and down and bear arms for their country for two years. By the time they'd finished with that, most of them had learned to be responsible adults.

CHAPTER 21: BUGS 'N RUGS.

God in His Infinite Mercy, at least since the time of Adam and Eve, makes his creatures so that they eventually wear out. Some bits wear out more quickly than others, partly because they get over-used or drop off maybe, and partly because some bits may be genetically faulty, like bad teeth or varicose veins. It ought also to be stated, as Mr Tinkler, the Lerwick dentist, pointed out sapiently on one occasion, that the original evolved human was designed to last about 35 to 40 years. Most folk's bits and pieces, and teeth, will do well enough for that long – provided they haven't been eating toffee all the time. But if humans have since taken to lasting about twice their original span, they shouldn't feel aggrieved if over-used bits drop off or rot. Or have to be replaced with plastic bits or transplants.

So anyway, after 14 years employment in the tropical opposite of my natural environment, bits were wearing out. Because I was still as keen as ever, I ignored all the signs as long as possible, but eventually Maisie said: "You need a rest, Herbie." She was trying to tell me I wasn't the superhuman British provincial Governor of Boys' Own Paper legend that I secretly fancied myself. "I've seen the signs often enough," she said. "Take Auntie Maisie's word for it. Before it's too late. In this heat you could go out like a light." "I hear dee," I said.

"You could go out like a light," said Maisie.

It seldom takes much to persuade a typical male that he's really ill. I went to Dr Hameed at the Hospital for a second opinion. "You need a break" he said. "You mean I'm not really ill," I said, trying to keep the disappointment out of my voice. But the good doctor knew his job too well. "Don't get me wrong," he said. "You could go out like a light. Especially in this heat." Later, when I thought about it, I reckoned he and Maisie had been in collusion.

A change, they say, is as good as a rest. So I decided on a change. Generally, I just felt a bit lacking in energy, uninspired, pains in the chest, grey hairs, the usual. Doing something different should be just the thing to get me firing on all cylinders again.

Among the regularly recurring little problems in the Gwelo in-tray was an up-country hill tribe called the Rugs. Yeah, that really was their name. Obviously the word meant something different in their lingo: like maybe, "Super-virile unconquerable He-Men" or words to that effect. I mean the word "Scots" originally didn't mean: Ginger-haired, kilt-wearing, bagpipe-playing Tarzans. It originally meant just "Robbers". Pretty accurate then.

For years these Rugs lived lives of exemplary tranquility, were only seen now and again when they came down-river in their canoes to do a little shopping. They attended their mission churches every Sunday, sang hymns with a will, and their tribal elders complied to the letter with the simple dictates of the government of President for Life Mzuzikele and his faithful provincial Governor. But from time to time in recent years and for no known reason they all suddenly went on the rampage. It was a phenomenon in fact that reminded me of old Tom Rhubarb at Mid Yell. For most of the year Tom was a perfectly sober, obliging, God-fearing fine old Christian boady, but suddenly and for no obvious cause he would get seriously and riotously blootered, continuing thus for some time, usually till all the money ran out. Then he reverted to normal, quite as if nothing untoward had happened. This, I rather think, is not totally uncommon elsewhere in the Shetland Islands, and, no doubt nowadays gives psychologists, sociologists, alcohologists and many another Council-employed expert plenty to think about. Heaven forbid that all the experts should find themselves with nothing to do. Where would we be without them?

Anyway, the Rugs had taken to going on the rampage at irregular intervals. In the pre-colonial past, this sort of thing made little difference as all the tribes lived more or less at war with their neighbours. When the Belgians took over in Upswapo, they took the opportunity of any tribal unrest to shoot as many of them as they could manage, sometimes even organising shoots as if they were pheasants or grouse. When, unlamented, the Belgians sloped off in a hurry, there was so much mayhem that any contribution the Rugs made hardly amounted to a serious threat to anything, law and order having disappeared anyway as modern weaponry flooded in, transforming traditional tribal squabbles into ethnic cleansing. So it was only since the imposition of firm government that this became a problem to be dealt with, and dealt with, of course by little me.

A trip up-river was therefore my idea of a holiday from the pressures of middle age in affairs of state. A fortnight in Tenerife might have been better, except, of course, it's full of Shetlanders eating full Scottish breakfasts.

I suppose, in my flaccid state, I had fondly imagined this would be an interesting river journey through a little-known part of central Africa, with a sort of Durbar at the end of it, whereat I would meet and greet Rug chieftains in ceremonial style, dish out medals and impressive certificates, and have a bit of a chinwag over dishes of favourite traditional nosh – spam fritters were usually top of the list – and bowls of the local firewater. We would reach an agreement pleasing to President for Life Mzuzikele, whereby the Rugs would give up their anti-democratic practices, chieftains and elders would receive satisfyingly large increases in the bank accounts and that would be that. But it was not to be quite like that.

It was, I believe, the late Baron of Ravenstone in his book "Grabola" (Noost Trilogy, vol 2) who had one of his characters say, *à propos* jungles that "Where there are no roads, there are many ways." Wise words indeed. Jungles are not impenetrable barriers to those who have always lived there. Quite the reverse. They are also, for folk like the Rugs vast and illimitable hunting grounds. Except where they have been opened up to exploit the timber or to dig mines, jungles have not greatly altered in modern times except inasmuch as the widespread political and tribal unrest has increased the numbers of armed groups wandering about in them. It's still the case that a native of the place with bow and arrows and a few spears can look after himself and his chums to pretty deadly effect even against government troops or white mercenaries, both of which though armed to the teeth, can easily get lost and ambushed.

The only modern road in Upswapo, the Barking-Thrush Inter Galactic Highway, running from Windsor to Rumbaba, lay well to the south of Gwelo. The only other main route, the great grey green greasy Urumguano was the one we now proposed to use. But even that was not going to be simple. The Rugs were semi-nomadic types. Sometimes they lived at home in their big jungle villages; at other times they took off for half a year or so, hunting well beyond the white-manmade political boundaries and into the uplands of eastern DRC. Their wanderings knew no bounds: DRC, Central African Republic (CAR), even the south western reaches of the Sudan, and northern Uganda. Normally, they caused no problems and the people they wandered among made no attempt to keep them out, but then sometimes, like old Tom Rhubarb, they ran amok.

The more I thought about the Rugs, the more I realised I had a lot to learn.

CHAPTER 22: JUMBO TROTTER SPILLS THE BEANS.

So in other words, the more I thought about it, the more preparations I found it necessary to make. I took myself off to Rumbaba to see what, if anything, was in government records there, and to sound out the innermost recesses of the learned minds of senior civil servants and university professors. Better even than that, I spent evenings with old chums at the reconstructed Queen of Heaven Nite Club Bar. If I'd stopped there with Maria and her ladies and given the Rugs the brush-off, I'd have been a lot healthier.

On my second night in town, I ran into Major de Landings, now well through his Seventies, but plainly benefitting from retirement in a warm climate. "Norman!" I cried, "So you haven't gone back to connubial bliss in dear old Bournemouth then."

"Damn right, dear boy!" replied the Major. "For a kick-off there's no place quite like Maria's there. Place is full of gays!"

As a chum of the President's and living now in a luxury bungalow in one of the posher suburbs of Rumbaba, the Major had the best of everything, including servants. Bonzo was not the man to forget old friends. I told him what I was about.

"Rugs, eh?" he said. "Damn queer lot if you ask me. Had an adjutant who was a Rug in the last show but one. Hard as nails these blighters. Drank like a fish but never showed it. Tell you what though, Herbie old fruit. Wasn't there a Rugs regiment in the Last War? They weren't just in Upswapo or the Congo, you know. Stretched across into the Sudan and Kenya what? Yes, I'm pretty sure there was you know: Queen's Own Rugs. For some totally unknown reason they had a depot in Bath. The Bath Rugs they were always called. Yes, I'm certain of it. In fact, d'you know, I believe m'late cousin Reggie served with them in Italy in '43 and '44. Damn fine bunch of men they were, is what Reggie said. Gone, alas, dear laddie, with all the rich, bright panoply of Empire. Now no more remembered than Pooter's Horse. But you'd expect their own people would remember them, what? The Bath Rugs. Yes, that was definitely it. An outfit like that, they can disband it and pay it off and send 'em all back to their native jungles, deserts and hillsides, but surely to God, Herbie, that really can't just be the end of the story, what? What? Drink up, dear heart!"

We drank, and had a damn fine evening one way or the other. The Major said he could probably find out more, and would let me have a note of anything that came through. And in the morning, as well as feeling my age – the Major seemed quite as brisk as ever – I knew I now had an extra reason for chasing up the Rugs.

I waited in Gwelo till the tail end of the rainy season up-country before setting off. The river and all its confusing tributaries were at their highest then so our little boats could take us as far up as Jinjah without much trouble, although the water was coming down at a fair rate of knots and you needed to keep the helm with the current. Jinjah, an ancient tribal settlement with records going back well before colonial times, was the official head village of the Rugs in Magongo territory but we found it nearly empty: only women, children and a few of the more geriatric tribal elders. The rest, they said, had gone hunting. How long since? Who knows? Many days. How long till back? Who knows? Many days. Did they go north? Up river? Maybe. Did they go by boat? Some of them.

We parked ourselves in the official guest house and waited to interview Ngwozo the Wise One, the chief Elder. You didn't just breeze in on Ngwozo and start asking him a lot of damn fool questions. That would have been the height of bad manners and totally counterproductive. At the same time, however, Ngwozo was in receipt of a Government pension as an official Elder. He could insist on his privileges, but not for long. There were always plenty candidates for the job of Elder: some of them were mere teenagers. The thing was to observe the proprieties.

It was while we were thus hanging around in Jinjah that Major de Landings' letter arrived. He had gone to some trouble to research the QOR (Queen's Own Rugs) and found they had a history that went back a lot further than the Second World War, in which they had also served with distinction in North Africa, Italy and finally in Germany in 1945.

The regiment had first seen the light of martial glory, explained the Major, in the 1890s, during the scramble by the European Powers for Central Africa when, as the Earl of Strathmurder's Irregulars, they had been charged by that nobleman with the task of seizing the headwaters of the Urumguano and holding them against all comers. This area remains their tribal HQ to this day. In discharge of this duty on his lordship's behalf, the Rugs had seen off the Belgians, French, Germans, Italians and a party of Japanese tourists which included the Crown Prince and Princess of Japan. So impressed was Queen Victoria on hearing report of this that she issued orders immediately and without further fuss and bother, regularising Lord Strathmurder's regiment as the QOR, and appointing as their Colonel-in-Chief HRH Princess Chrissie of Saxe-Mecklenburg-Gottorp, one of her lesser-known grand-daughters, married to Adolphus, Grand Duke of Saxe-Mecklenburg-Gottorp. During the First World War, the Rugs had fought the Germans in their Damaraland and Tanganyika colonies, and later served with great bravery at the third Battle of Ypres. Their unblemished record in WW2 I have already mentioned. After 1945, together with many other colonial and Indian Army regiments, they were disbanded: the days of Empire were ended: never again would such regiments be required to answer the call of the King-Emperor. A few of them, like my late adjutant, got themselves transferred to other outfits, but most went back home, put their uniforms and medals in a box under the bed and went back to being Rugs. They were, I rather think, pretty dischuffed, and I for one can well understand why.

But there was one saving grace, continued the Major, and this he had only learned about from an old regimental chum in Windsor. This chep, "Squiffy" Jumbo-Trotter of the old 60th Light Dragoons, whom the major had run into entirely accidentally one evening in the bar of the old Mango Club in Hospital Street, up behind the fire station if you know the place, had been able to tell him a few extra facts about the Bath Rugs – or Bath Plugs as he insisted on calling 'em (he wasn't called "Squiffy" for nothing) – that might otherwise have been forever forgotten, and that for the simple reason that his late sire, "Pongo" Jumbo-Trotter, had been a Colonel in the QOR during the Last War. Squiffy told how, some time during the First World War, Princess Chrissie and the Grand Duke had, as they say nowadays, "split up," perhaps due to the War, although of course, as Queen Victoria's granddaughter there was not the slightest question in those far-off days of them getting officially divorced. Some time in the 'Twenties, the Princess, who was still a comparatively young woman, came out to Kenya and settled on a large up-country plantation, where she became a member of the so-called "Happy Valley Set" and where she was always known as Lady Chrissie Mecklenburg. A great deal of tosh has been written about this rather innocuous set, who were more frivolous than vicious and almost certainly no more adulterous than anyone else then or now. Besides, the Princess took her responsibilites as Colonel-in-Chief of the Rugs very much to heart. Throughout this period, and all through the next War, she was tireless in her effort to raise funds and provide amenities for veteran Rugs who had suffered in the War. In fact, Squiffy said the good lady had never ceased in her efforts, holding dances, whist drives, tombola, garden fetes and car rallies – all to benefit the regiment, not just in Kenya but up into the Sudan, and elsewhere – all British in those days, of course. All her spare time was devoted to her QOR Welfare and Benevolent Committee (QORWAB). Well, not quite all perhaps, for sometime in the 'Thirties she gave birth to a daughter, Patricia – known as Trixie – who, of course, as her parents were still officially conjoined in wedlock was reckoned legit. Royal progeny. Squiffy said that he reckoned the Grand Duke wasn't in the least put out, as he was by then living happily with an SS aviator in a bijou flat in Berlin, just off the Theresienstadt if you know the place as it was before the War. He came good, in the end, however, did Adolphus,

for he was later hanged for his part in the bomb plot that blew the trousers off the dear Führer. As for who Trixie's father was, well of course, Squiffy said there was no end of suggestions at the time, the long term favourite being "Buffy" Strathmurder, who was a member of that set and certainly a lady's man of, as they say, epic proportions. At least no one for a moment thought it might be any of the servants.

"After the War," concluded the Major, "I haven't much more to relate. Obviously the Bath Plugs disbanded and Squiffy's esteemed pa was back in the UK and completely out of touch. Squiffy couldn't remember for the life of him where Princess Chrissie ended up. He had an idea she might have been offered a grace and favour residence by King George VI. She must have been gone by the time of the Kikuyu Emergency in the 'Fifties, he said. Besides, she'd have been pretty ancient by then. Gone alas, as the poet saith, like our Youth too soon. All the trappings of Empire. The Captains, and the Kings – and the Princesses – depart. Toodle Pip, Old Fruit. Hope you have a jolly trip up-river. N de L."

CHAPTER 23: NGWOZO.

Ngwozo the Wise One, once he got revved up with a beaker or two of his special brew, had a fair bit to tell us about his tribe. But first we had to assure him we were not on any sort of punishment trip. The only times the Belgians had visited places like Jinjah had been either to massacre the inhabitants, rob them of everything they possessed or enslave them for labour on their rubber plantations or down the mines. As far as old people like Ngwozo were concerned, all white men were potential Belgians. He was probably right. I tried to explain that although I was coloured a nasty light greeny-grey colour, I was a faithful servant of President Mzuzikele and had fought alongside him to free Upswapo from exploiters.

"The Rugs have gone hunting?" I said.

"Some hunting, some fighting," said Ngwozo, "Fighting where?" I asked. "Not in Upswapo. not in Magongo," said the Elder. "Far away. No problem for President Mzuzikele. They come back four, maybe five months." "In DCR?" I asked. "In Chilubambashi," said Ngwozo, naming a place I had never heard of. I turned to Jake Mlumbo, the guy I relied on for all geographic information, an officer of the Gwelo Regiment and as keen as mustard.

"The only Chilubambashi I know is right up in the northern border of the DCR," said Jake. "Up in the Bamakwe Highlands on the Sudan frontier. It's a long way from anywhere, but at this time of year with the rivers high you could maybe get as far as Ushwara up the Ushwara tributary. After that, we'd have to hoof it, though perhaps it's easier going the higher up you get."

"Have you been there, Jake?" I asked him.

"No Sah!" said Jake. "And I can't think of anyone I know who has."

"Why they go Chilubambashi?" I asked Ngwozo.

"Every year go there," he replied.

"So far away?" I said.

"Birth place of Rug nation," he said.

I asked Jake to try and elucidate this further in his native language, although as Jake was an Anugu and the Rugs weren't, it was arguable whether he would open up more to him than to me in our stilted English. But Jake rattled off in Rug for a while, and Ngwozo, after a refill of his beaker, definitely became a bit more forthcoming. These tribes by the way were not just linguistically different. You could tell them apart easily enough: the Magongo tribes, the Anugu, were a dark chocolate brown in skin colour, whereas the Rugs, being I suppose originally a northern Nilotic tribe like the southern Sudan tribes, were an amazing blue-black.

Sgt. Mlumbo questions Elder Ngwozo.

Both types were a damn sight better colour than light greeny grey.

"Okay," said Jake after a prolonged session. "He's keeping something back I think, but this Chilubambashi place is sort of like the centre of the universe for the Rugs and has been from time immemorial. They think the spirits of all their ancestors are gathered near there. They're Christians now, he says, but before that they believed that the God who began the Rugs stepped out of the sky onto some hilltop there, near Chilubambashi. Many hundreds of years ago, apparently, the Rugs ruled some sort of empire centred on Chilubambashi. Their King, or in some cases Queen, had his palace near there. Again, according to their traditions, this ruler was supposed to be White, which probably means he came there from Egypt. It is possible maybe: the Ancient Egyptians penetrated far south into the Sudan. What is there today? There is only one way we're going to find that out, Sah!"

"Thank you, Jake," I said. "You're right of course. Did you get any inkling about what he might be keeping back?"

"There's something called Wuluwulu, some sort of narcotic that grows in due season on this Bamakwe mountainside, perhaps some sort of mushroom. Pretty harmless stuff I think. I've heard about it before from some of our men. They collect it at certain times of year. That's another reason they go there I suppose. If they gather it at the right time they can smoke it or something like that."

"Could it make 'em into rampaging warriors?" I asked.

Jake laughed. "Is that what magic mushrooms do to British hippies?" he asked.

"What about the fighting he mentioned?" I asked, but Ngwozo had said no more about that. It was my turn to ask him: "Who do the Rugs fight when they go to Chilubambashi?"

"Bad mans," said the Elder. "Is mighty far from Magongo. No problem for President. In DCR all mans fight each other. Bad mans come there. Rugs, kill."

"And eat probably," whispered Jake.

Ngwoza hadn't given much away, but just a little more than he probably meant to. Why did the Bad Mans – by which he meant white men – come all that way in the first place? It was a helluva long journey for magic mushrooms. Now there wasn't the least doubt about it: we were going to have to pay a visit to Chilubambashi. And Ngwozo, as government sponsored Elder, was going to have to supply us with reliable guides.

CHAPTER 24: MADAME MAFUDI EXTENDS A WELCOME.

It was now I made the first mistake. Now that we were extending our itinerary to far distant Chilubambashi, I ought to have waited a little longer at Jinjah till extra troops could be brought up. It wouldn't have taken long, and another thirty added to the twenty we had would have been plenty. But Wise Old Ngwozo advised against it: once the Urumguano and its tributaries started to go down, he said, we'd never get anywhere near Ushwara by boat, and trudging there through verdant jungle would take weeks. Besides, I was supposed to be having a rest cure: the more men you have, the more supply problems and so on. So I decided against it. Twenty men can live off the country no bother.

Mistake number two followed fast on the heels of number one. I decided we'd change into civvies and leave our uniforms with Elder Ngwozo: sooner or later we were going to have to carry everything on our backs, so the less inessential clobber we had the better. Besides, unofficial bands of men were common enough rambling around in these parts: there was no effective central government, rival private armies roamed the whole country and over in the Sudan, there had been an almost continuous civil war in the South since the British left in 1956. One more unofficial band of wanderers would cause no political stushie, whereas a uniformed unit of the Magongo National Army might be deemed an invasion force and cause complications. That was the thinking behind it. Was I truly getting past it, or was it something in Ngwozo's maraka?

We made good progress along the upper Urumguano, locating and following the Ushwara tributary with the aid of our guides. Thereafter the going got rougher, the Ushwara being full of obstacles: cataracts being the worst but there were also plenty of overhanging trees and creepers, not to mention crocodiles and the odd submerged hippo. It wasn't the best sort of waterway to tip up in. The further we went, the worse it got, and without the two guides we would have been in dire straits, especially now that the rains were past and the water level dropping. It was a relief when we eventually reached Ushwara, and drew up our three boats onto the bank to await our return.

Ushwara was unquestionably a hicksville sort of place, made up of basic jungle huts, a Head Man's tin shack, a couple of tin shops, a tin mission church, and, incongruously, a ramshackle hotel still retaining its original name, The King Leopold. There weren't many guests. The proprietrix, a large lady who introduced herself as Madame Mafudi, greeted us warmly and we bedded down for the night, though the resident buglife prevented much peaceful slumber.

The Head Man was there next morning, preventing our setting off as he questioned us about the purpose of our visit. It took a while because, now that we were in the DRC, the official language was French and despite the well-meaning efforts of Miss Peatrose from Bressay, my ability with this lingo was nil. Once again I had to rely on Sgt Jake Mlumbo to do his best, which he did with a will, but soon found it easier going in his native dialect, the Head Man's own proving partly compatible therewith. A bit of confusion was unavoidable however, and the Head Man appeared to find his worst suspicions confirmed. At first he thought we were mercenaries, then despite our trying to explain we were a fact-finding mission from the regional government at Gwelo trying to locate the whereabouts of some of our errant citizens, the Rugs, he became convinced that what he had in front of him was a plain-clothes, armed reconnaissance unit of the Magongoese Armed Forces, proof, if any were needed, that President Mzuzikele was planning an invasion, and an annexation of this part of the DRC, just like he'd done in Upswapo fourteen years previously. I told him this was absurd – or attempted to tell him – and that no one in his right mind would want to take over his lawless, terrorist-infested province, especially someone sensible like President Mzuzikele, who had made such a success of Magongo that it was the envy of Africa.

The upshot of all this was he declared we would all have to remain here in Ushwara under strict surveillance until a senior government officer could come up from the provincial capital – about 250km away – to make a decision on this weighty matter. "How long will that take?" I remonstrated. He shrugged. "That is my decision," he said. In French. It might be good news for Madame Mafudi, but a total no-no for the rest of us. Given the state of the country, it would take the senior government officer months, if he ever set out at all with the hefty protection he was no doubt going to require before he took a step out of his office.

Fortunately, however, I had taken advice before setting out about how one ought to deal with DRC officials. Thus I had also taken with me a useful wad of US Dollars, and later in the day I called upon the Head Man and made him a modest gift. That evening, he and I and Sgt Mlumbo and a couple of our NCOs foregathered on the verandah of his shack and partook of a few noggins from his plentifully stacked paraffin fridge, before moving on back to the The King Leopold where, the Head Man assured us, Madame Mafudi ran a very acceptable house of gentlemen's entertainments. I wouldn't say I knew much about King Leopold except that he was by all accounts a bastard of epic proportions as far as colonialist atrocities went, but during the rest of that evening, we soon discovered that there was a lot more interesting life in his Hotel than bedbugs. It maybe wasn't quite up to the Queen of Heaven in class, but it lacked for very little in variety. It was certainly too good for a dump like Ushwara, and during the course of the evening I made a point of telling that to the ever-accommodating Madame Mafudi. In elegant French – well, it might have been elegant Serbo-Croat for all I'd know – the good lady explained through Sgt Mlumbo that the dear old place had certainly seen better days, but she and her girls were ever prepared to bend over backwards to oblige their clientele. They still served a decent chilled Stella Artois, and there were portraits of the current Belgian Monarch in all the bedrooms. People appreciated these little touches of style, she said, dating as they did from a more gracious age of slavery, mass killings and capitalist exploitation on a truly heroic scale. Fortunately, the more she drank, the more Madame Mafudi attempted to speak in English, which she had picked up, she explained, from many customers of distinction, especially the famous soldier of fortune, Mr Ludo. Did I know him? He was a real English gent, she said. I told her I knew of him and had come close to meeting him on more than one occasion during the Upswapo War, but he had given us the

slip after blowing up the national Bank and an American Admiral.

"Quel gent!" she said approvingly. "He seems to have disappeared now," I said. "Disappeared?" she exclaimed disdainfully. "Not at all mon General! Ee 'as not disappeared! Ee was in 'ere last week. And 'ees men! Zey come in regular. On their way to Chilubambashi."

Blimey! I thought. What's all this about? "That's just where we're heading for," I told her. Perhaps I was going to meet Ludo at last. She looked at me a bit more pensively. "You go Chilubambashi? To ze long lost Empire of ze Roogs? Ees long way to go, Mon General. Long Way. Up mountains. Many troubles. There you meet Great White Queen. Maybe no. And maybe you meet Meestair Blotts. You tell Meestair Blotts from me: Madame Mafudi and ze girls looking forward *très avidement* to meeting 'im again." Whoever Mr Blotts was, what ever he was up to in Chilubambashi, he had plainly made a lasting impression on the ladies of The King Leopold. Who was this Lion of the boudoir?

I draw a veil over the rest of the evening's proceedings. In the morning, it all seemed a bit vague, though one thought rattled alarmingly loud in my troubled mind: What were we going to do with only twenty men if confronted in a remote spot by Ludo and Co? And I'd already committed my third mistake: Why in Heaven's Holy Name had I told half the population of Ushwara that we were headed for Chilubambashi? There's only one answer to that: Drink.

CHAPTER 25: RAMON HITCHES A LIFT.

Three hours hard hacking along heavily overgrown jungle tracks took most of the after effects of a night at the King Leopold out of our systems. Now we had left the river behind, everything had to be carried, including emergency supplies, weaponry and tents. We shot game during the day and did all right in that department: a nice piece of fried monkey goes down a treat after a hard day's yomping. By the end of Day Five, we were starting to ascend into the Bamakwe: the vegetation was thinning out and the air becoming mercifully fresher. By Day Eight we were in different terrain altogether, wooded upland hill country with dense, wooded steep valleys. From the hill tops you could see it stretching far away before you, a great relief from the ceaseless sweaty claustrophobia of the jungle. There were mountains too, their tops wreathed in high, wispy clouds, and here and there from the valley sides came the thin smoke trails of little villages hidden among the trees. We were in the land of the Rugs, and I could see why they liked to get back there. Mountain lions and giraffes were to be seen. The air was fresh and clear and it was no longer swelteringly hot. At night we needed to unpack a few blankets.

More important than blankets, however, were sentries. Till now we had managed to rest up in habitations or on our boats anchored in midstream. Now I posted a couple of men on watch throughout the night, two so that at least one of them might be awake, and both of 'em changed every hour. That this was not an unnecessary precaution became clear on the very first night, when the sentries became aware of someone padding about just beyond the perimeter of the camp. The sentry shouted at them to halt or be shot, and when the prowlers took off the sentries fired and at least one of them was probably winged, as there was a sharp involuntary yelp. Next night it happened again and this time they'd come prepared, for they fired back, automatic fire not bows and arrows, so that all of us leapt from our respective sacks and started firing at random. This exchange in the pitch dark – as well as threatening heart attacks to the jungle wild-life – persuaded me that despite the beauty of the countryside it wasn't just an ideal place for a spot of camping.

In the morning we found two of our visitors: one was stone dead, and one was seriously injured with a bullet in his back. "Doc" Michael Ajang, our medical orderly, had a look at him. His prognosis was that either he could try and cut the bullet out – which could well prove lethal – or the guy was going to die anyway. I told him to get on with it, so he gave him a shot of morphine and commenced cutting, while the rest of us erected a makeshift shelter around them and tried to keep the flies off. It was a messy job and took about an hour before Michael had the bullet out, everything sewn up as best he could and a field dressing in place. The guy was plainly not going to be up and running through the jungle at midnight again, for some considerable time.

Neither of these intruders was a native of the place: to me they looked like Cubans, and pretty ugly ones at that, but as they were in no position to enlighten us, I decided to make for the nearest village. I had no intention of spending another night in the open anyway. We buried the dead guy, made a stretcher, loaded our unconscious chum onto it and headed downhill.

Here at Gumbwamalubu village, our arrival created a bit of a stir and the natives came out to meet us. "Do you have a medical centre?" I asked through Jake Mlumbo. "No," they said. "and we don't want this Bad Man anyway. You should have left him to die." "Take me to your Head Man," I said.

The upshot was we would leave the wounded guy with the Head Man, who looked totally dischuffed at this unexpected privilege. However, when we were about to depart, having ascertained where the next village was, Doc Michael went to take a final check on his patient and found he had regained consciousness. His wound showed no sign of festering and the man, though still fevered, was not delirious. Michael was pleased with his progress and thought that if the man could just rest here in the village instead of being trundled around on a makeshift stretcher over rough country, he had a distinctly improved chance of living to murder, rape and pillage another day. However, we all make mistakes, and Michael made the mistake of telling the guy we were now about to bid him a fond farewell and leave him at the village. Immediately, the man's condition took a turn for the worse. "No leave me here with Roogs!" he pleaded, the sweat pouring from his body. "They keel me at once you go! No leev me 'ere! No leev me!"

"Bugger," said Michael, and came to fetch me. I went to see the fellow. He was no oil painting and no spring chicken, but then neither was I. "You Commandante?" he asked. "Yeah," I said. "No leev me 'ere, Commandante!" he whined. "They keel me. I too seek to fight. They keel me easy. Bang Bang! You take me weeth you, Yes? I be good boy! No problemos! I beg you Commandant!"

I looked at him: he was thin, his clothes filthy, his face lined and hard, like the killer he was. He was well through his fifties. "What's your name Comrade?" I asked. "Ramon, Commandante," he said, gazing at me with the wide eyes of the seriously unwell. "I be good boy! Doctor say I get better. You save my life. Ramon serve you good."

"Sure you will, pal," I said. He was in no state to argue. It had been clear from the first that the Rugs of Gumbwamalubu wanted him dead, and there was nothing to stop them shooting him as soon as we left town. Even his own chums had left him for dead. To the Rugs he was vermin, and to his friends he was expendable. So I decided to take him with us, at least as far as the next village. If Christ's Gospel means anything, it means helping guys like Ramon make it through to the next day, if you get the chance. Father MacFadzeon would have been proud of me, smarmy bastard. God knows, Ramon was no weight to carry.

The track widened and soon we began to see the ruts of vehicle tyres, then not just ruts, but big potholes, sure signs of heavy vehicles on unmade roads. Next we were hearing the unmistakable roar and whine of a slow-moving, labouring lorry bumping and grinding along some way in front of us. A mammy wagon hauled into view, painted all over in bright designs and slogans, crammed with humanity, old folk hanging on for dear life, young mothers with their babies wrapped up in cloth, and tied on their backs, men discussing everything volubly in loud voices, plus their goats, sheep, poultry and mothers-in-law. We got off the track to let it pass, but the driver ground to a halt and leaned out.

"Where you go?" he asked. I told him we were headed for the next village. "But where you go after that?" he probed. I told him we were trying to get to Chilubambashi. "Then you in luck, my friend!" he announced grinning, "I go Gombwamalubu. Then tomorrow early morning, Jesus Willing, I go back again Chilubambashi, through all villages. You stay next village and I pick you up there tomorrow morning. From there to Chilubambashi plenty cheap. I keep places for you and all you people if book now. Understand?"

This seemed like a godsend. Perhaps that had been a good move picking up Ramon. "How much for 21 men and one guy on stretcher? He's got to stay lying down?" The driver told me the price and I argued it down a little because that was the way they did it. "It's a deal, Comrade," I said and we shook hands vigorously. "I put sick fellow up on roof, with all the bundles, and tie him on there," he said. "He be plenty fine up there." So saying, he crashed into gear, and his passengers, who had been discussing all this from every angle throughout our negotiation, tightened their grip on various parts of the lorry and lurched off happily on the rutted road to Gombwamalubu, disappearing eventually in a cloud of thick dust, plaintive goat noises and chicken cheeps.

So that's how eventually we would get to Chilubambashi: in style if not in comfort. That first night, waiting on the lorry's return, we all had a peaceful rest in the rest house attached to the Head Man's hut. Ramon continued to progress and could move a little though still not strong enough to get up and go about for himself. The thought of travelling sixty miles or more tied on a mammy wagon roof in no way disturbed him. He was just glad to be alive. He had never lived a pampered life so hardship came naturally to him. A bit like the old-time Shetland ships biscuits, and unlike today's Cheesy Wotsits.

Everyone was looking forward to getting a lift the rest of the way, not having to hoof it any further with hefty packs and weapons to carry, so there was a general mood of mild rejoicing when the mammy wagon lurched into the village next morning in good time. A few passengers got off and we squeezed on, greeting and being greeted by those on board in friendly fashion. The only problem was the driver insisted the rule was: No Weapons On Board, so, after a bit of argie-bargie, this meant we had to put ours up top along with the assorted spears, rifles, muzzle-loaders and pangas already up there. Few men went anywhere without one. Plainly, allowing folk to carry such hardware on board the lorry would have been asking for trouble. Off we lurched and soon we were involved in multiple conversations with our fellow passengers in a variety of languages, or bits of languages rather.

It was not unlike the old Overland in the Shetland North Isles, especially because it called in at all the little villages en route, and often enough the driver and sometimes passengers as well, would descend for prolonged consultations with the natives. It was in other words, a relic of a more gracious age, where civilized congress and the leisurely interchange of news and views took precedence over speed and comfort.

CHAPTER 26: AMBUSH.

Our only indication that something was up was when the driver started changing down in the middle of nowhere. By leaning far out over the side of the lorry you could see, some way up ahead, two military jeeps parked across the road. The lorry ground to a halt. A cacophony of querulous voices broke out in the back, like a hen-coop whose inhabitants sense the fox is near. Suddenly, the whole place was swarmimg with men in assorted army gear, waving AK 47s. "Out! Out!" they shouted. "Ev' body out!"

The passengers fell suddenly silent. Some had seen it before: all had heard of it. A baby started crying. "Out! Out!" they roared and started firing into the air to reinforce their message. Even had we had our own weapons to hand, there was no way we could have started firing at them with all the civilians packed around us. We got down. "Magongo Army bastards over here!" they shouted, waving us off onto the right side of the track. "Rest over here! Other side! Hands up! Keep hands up!" We did as we were told. What else was there to do? You tell me.

A tall white man, in a British officer's battered cap came up to me. "Captain Voar?" he asked. He didn't hold out a hand. "Yes," I said. "We meet at last, Dear Boy," he said in a perfect Oxford accent. "I'm Ludo. Just stand back a bit over this way, will you?" He motioned me to stand back over near the lorry, where a beefy guy grabbed me and kept me there. Then

Ludo

"Okay," said Ludo nonchalantly to his NCO. Without any warning, his men suddenly opened fire at point blank range, firing round after round into our defenceless men. They died there in front of my eyes while I stood in the grip of the big guy.

"You really shouldn't meddle in other people's business, you know," Ludo said. "Not wise." He walked back across the track, to where his men were inspecting their handiwork, took out his revolver and began shooting those he thought might not be quite dead. All our gallant lads. Sgt Jake Mlumbo, M.O. Michael Ajang and the rest. Gone to rotting meat in seconds.

"You utter filth," I blurted out. I was almost too sick to speak. "I'll see you hang for this."

Ludo laughed. "You're going nowhere, Captain," he said. "I only kept you out of it because you're English." "I'm not English," I said. "Well, Jocko then," he said. "Next best thing." "I'm a Shetlander," I said. He stared at me. "Good God," he said. "One of them's more than enough."

But the shooting hadn't quite finished.

Suddenly a rapid and continuous outbreak of automatic fire sprayed the area where Ludo's men were standing. They started running, falling over, writhing about. I saw Ludo himself jump in agony and clutch his face, but that's all I saw for the big guy who still held me hurled me to the ground and threw himself on top of me. It was like a piano falling on you. I had no idea what was happening or where the firing was coming from until it dawned on me as I lay there winded, gasping for breath and with my face pressed into the dirt: it had to be Ramon. He didn't want for weapons up there, and in the horror of what had been happening no one had given him a thought. Almost certainly in great pain, he had wriggled out of his coverings and the straps that held him in place and got to one of our AK 47s. Now he was using it on his own former comrades, repaying his debt of gratitude to us in the best way he could.

But not for long. Someone, probably Ludo's NCO, Sgt Boma, must have chucked a grenade into the back of the lorry, for the next thing was a hellish explosion followed by an even bigger one as the fuel tanks blew up. These wagons carried a lot of fuel for there were no petrol stations anywhere along their route. It was a devastating explosion, with a wave of intense heat, bits of lorry flying everywhere. It was the end of Ramon, and the end of the big guy lying on top of me: if he hadn't been there, it would also have been the end of me, for we had been nearest the truck. The heat of the blast had roasted the guy's back like a badly charred cocktail sausage, melting his clothes and setting his hair alight. The first I saw of it all was when he rolled off me screaming and writhing in agony. Then he lay silent. All around I could see a scene like one of those old Dutch paintings of Hell: the skeletal, blackened remains of the lorry, guys writhing, others wandering hopelessly about, the wagon passengers, most of whom had been far enough away not to be roasted alive shrieking and some on their knees praying to God for deliverance. And in among it all like Lucifer himself, Ludo, blood pouring from a wound to his face, but upright and cool.

"Well done, Sergeant," he managed to say to Boma. "Just go and get the First Aid box out of our jeep will you? Some of the lads look in need of patching up."

"Sah!" shouted Boma, and ran off.

Within little more than an arm's length away from me lay the roasted remains of the big guy. In amongst the charred remnants of his clothing was his pistol. No one was watching: everyone had troubles of his own. I reached out quickly and grabbed it, continuing to lie face down. I stuck it in the front of my shirt. To kill Ludo was my sole ambition in this life.

They began collecting up their dead and injured, laying out the former, patching up the latter and carrying the worst cases to the jeeps. They came for the big man, I staggererd to my feet, hunched over, and went to sit at the roadside as if only just regaining consciousness. They left me there, some of them fetching shovels and spades from the Jeeps, which they handed to the fittest looking among the passengers and told them: "Dig." Then they stood by and hit them, to make them dig quicker. From time to time they made them change over so that the pace didn't slacken. The passengers dug like they wanted to get to Oz without delay: they were scared the same would happen to them as they'd just seen happen to my men. In a very short time, the pit was ready. They dumped all the bodies in it. "Now fill it in!" Ludo said. "Quick!"

When the pit was full and levelled off, the passengers went back and huddled with their own little group, thankful I guess that they hadn't been shot and tipped in with the others. Ludo went across to them with Sgt Boma. He had a dressing over one side of his face and was leaning on a stick. They looked very very scared as he approached. "Listen!" he ordered, and Boma proceeded to translate his massage into Rug. "You know nothing about any of this. You never saw anything. You not know where any fellows buried. Lorry blown up by gangsters. They steal all your stuff, then blow up lorry. Get it? If any of you speak about this we will come in night and kill you just like we kill these fellows good. And then we kill your children, and your parents and all your village. Understand?"

"Yes, Sah!" they all said in English, as if trying to humour him. "We no tell nobody, Sah!"

While he was speaking to them, Ludo had his back to where I was sitting. I reckoned I wouldn't get a better chance. Most of his men were back at the jeeps. I raised the pistol. Then something very hard split into my head. That's all I knew for a very long time.

CHAPTER 27: BASKET CASE.

I reckon I was unconscious for three or four days. Obviously, some bastard had been a lot closer to me than I knew. I woke up in what can only be described as a filthy cell, legs chained to the wall, the only light coming from a tiny, barred window high up near the roof. I had a very bad headache and my head seemed to be covered with blood. Wherever I was, it wasn't the Grand Hotel, Lerwick.

I spent longer here than I can accurately estimate, all of it in near darkness, and punctuated only by the door opening twice a day and a large man coming in with a tin bowl of what I took to be maize porridge, and a plastic bottle of water. It was a monotonous diet, but better than starving. Three months? Three years? Who knows? It was not the happiest time. Worse than the filth and the head pain was the endless nagging certainty that I was responsible for the deaths of my twenty men. If it is the case that every guy comes to one fateful event in his life that suddenly tells him: That's it, the glory days are over, chum, there's nothing now but running downhill, then that was it for me. I've never been the same again, that's for sure. If I'd brought those extra men, if I'd kept my mouth shut at Madame Mafudi's, if this and if that... Day after day, sitting alone in the half light with the same thoughts and reflections running through my head: It wasn't great. Depression, I suppose. What they used to call Self Pity.

Just when I was beginning to think Jesus had forgotten me, the door opened one day at an unscheduled time and a woman came in. "Mistah Voar?" she asked. "Yes," I croaked, the old vocal chords lacking exercise. "I'm Grace Malumbwe," she said. She could not have sounded sweeter if she'd been the Queen of Heaven.

"What can I do for you, Grace?" I asked.

"Not much, by the looks of you," she replied. She searched around and found a stool: it had been out of range for me with the chains on my legs so I'd always just sat on the floor amongst the cockroaches and other tasty wildlife. Cockroaches, I reckoned, were good for you if your diet lacked protein. They were my equivalent of five fruits a day. Grace had a little basket with her. In it were biscuits, some bits of roast chicken and an open tin of sardines. "For you," she said. I have never yet dined at the

Dorchester, but no bonzo dinner anywhere could ever taste as good as that. "Jesus be praised!" I said when I'd finished – it didn't take me long. "Amen to that, Mistah Voar!" said Grace.

"What exactly are you doing here, Grace?" I asked. "How did you persuade the guard to let you in?"

She laughed. "Him?" she said. "He big softy. I no have bother with him." Then she told me who she was.

Grace's friend Mlende had been a passenger on the mammy wagon. During the peaceful part of the journey, she had been in conversation with one of our men. She'd asked him about Ramon up on the roof. The soldier had told Mlende how Ramon had got himself shot trying to raid our camp, how I'd ordered MO Ajang to operate on him, how we'd taken him with us instead of leaving him at Gombwamalubu. What Mlende hadn't told the soldier was that Ramon was her sister's husband. When, many weeks later, Mlende and her sister heard that I was locked up in poor conditions, they decided to see if they could do something to help. Grace had volunteered to do the legwork because she was bolder than the other two. So helping Ramon had been one of the few sensible things I'd done.

"Where am I, Grace?" I asked. "Where are you?" she repeated. "In jail, of course. In Chilubambashi jail. Did you think this was a hotel?" She laughed, shaking her head. It was news to me.

"What am I supposed to be guilty of?" I asked. "How can I be kept in jail so long without trial?"

"No trials in Chilubambashi," she said. "Anyone Mistah Ludo no like goes to jail. If they lucky. Otherwise they get shot. Bang Bang! Here in Chiluba is Ludo's Law."

"What about the government Head Man?" I asked.

"Mistah Ludo," she said. "He Head Man here. Everything controlled by Mistah Ludo. It's not so bad. As long as you keep in good with Mistah Ludo. They keep out all the riff-raff," she laughed. "Some things good, some things bad. As long as you no interfere with Ponka you be all right."

"Ponka?" I asked. She stared at me. "You gotta lot to learn, Mistah Voar." she said. She got up. "I gotta go. No want Jailer Man to get trouble.

I come back next week, God Willing."

Then, incredibly, filthy and festering as I was, she bent down and kissed me. "You keep smilin' Honey!" she said. At last I'd met a real life Christian. It looked to me as if the BVM was alive and living in Chilubambashi.

Herbie meets a Christian.

CHAPTER 28: KIBUGOMA.

Grace was a regular visitor after that. Like most ladies, she had a comprehensive knowledge of all that was going on in her own backyard. I gathered more facts about the Rugs from her than we ever gleaned traipsing through mile after mile of their territory. Or, as Mother used to say, one half-decent woman knows more than a regiment of men.

Up behind Chilubambashi, explained Grace, rose Kwakibu, the holy mountain of the Rugs or so they believed before the missionaries came and showed them the error of their ways. On its lower slopes in due season grew a unique plant which they call Wuluwulu. It was mildly narcotic and hallucinogenic. You could smoke it when dried, or boil it up in an infusion and drink it. It generally made you feel a bit better. It was recommended by native healers for a variety of human ailments: women's problems, infertility, bad backs, toothache, old age, etc, etc, etc. Traditionally it had been regarded as a gift from their gods, who were said to live higher up Kwakibu.

They were not the only ones to live there. In an inaccessible valley not far from the summit, usually wreathed in clouds, was said to be Kibugoma, the ancient fortress-palace of the Supreme Lord of the Rugs, known as the Great White King or Great White Queen, descended in theory from the original Creator of the World, Kibu, who had stepped from Heaven onto the newly created Earth by way of the mountain top.

Kibugoma

These rulers, during the ancient period when the Rugs ruled over a wide area of central Africa, were white because Kibu was white, and possibly because they were descended from the ancient Egyptians. As a theory there was nothing wrong with this, except that when the first white men began arriving in the nineteenth century, the Rugs ran to greet them with open arms and gifts of food, drink, nubile virgins and other things suitable for welcoming messengers of the gods.

When, all too soon, these godly types turned out to be mere Belgians and other white trash, the Rugs realised too late that life was no longer that simple. They were soon split between different colonies and different colonial masters, the British – on the initiative of the Earl of Strathmurder – offering them the opportunity to display their martial skills as a separate unit, the Queens Own Rugs (previously Strathmurder's Irregulars). This, besides obtaining brave warriors on the cheap for the British, at least allowed the Rugs to maintain their ancient status as a fighting race. When, as previously detailed, Princess Chrissie became their Colonel-in-Chief, they were wholly won over, for none of their tribal rivals had any such distinction and it meant that once again they had a Great White Queen in place of the last of their native rulers who had been killed in action against the British. When the Princess later came and dwelt among them in Africa and devoted most of her energies to fundraising, it pleased them even better. To be in the QOR was deemed at least as good as their previous autonomy. It was therefore a blow for the tribe when, after World War 2 the Regiment was disbanded. Lady Chrissie remained in Africa however, and was instrumental in securing the regimental funds – a considerable fortune, much of which she had raised herself – for the Rugs when the War Office in London was intent on absorbing it all for their own nefarious purposes. A committee of senior QOR officers was set up with herself as chairwoman, and called the Dergue, after the Rugs' ancient tribal parliament. Their mission was to find the best project to maintain Rug traditions. As time went by and it became pretty clear that the European colonialists were on their way out, this Dergue decided to use the funds to resuscitate Kibugoma and install the Princess there as their Great White Queen. By this time, however, – the late 'Fifties, I suppose – the lady herself, while retaining her spirit and distinction, was becoming elderly and frail. She had acquired an experienced male nurse as an essential member of her staff, and from this point on she became gradually more eccentric. As well as the Kibugoma Project, various mining companies were hired to prospect for minerals, but when the Congo broke up into civil war, escalating insecurity put an end to this effort. Some time in the 'Sixties, a hush-hush British military team descended on Kibugoma by helicopter via Uganda and removed Princess Chrissie despite the protests and opposition of her staff. She was taken home to England to be reunited with her relations and given a small apartment in Kensington Palace for the few remaining years of her memorable life. It is doubtful if she appreciated their concern, but someone in the very highest authority had ordered it and no doubt from their point of view it was most needful. One cannot after all leave grand-daughters of Queen Victoria lying around on remote African hillsides amid scenes of colonial disintegration, tribal violence and general confusion. Not British.

Exit Princess Chrissie of Saxe-Mecklenburg-Gottorp. The Rugs once again took it hard. Especially the Dergue. All their efforts at soldiering on seemed to be thwarted by higher powers.

Then they had an unexpected stroke of luck. Had Kibu the Wonder God finally returned to his sacred mountain?

CHAPTER 29: TRIXIE PULLS IT OFF

Trixie Mecklenburg had been brought up to fend for herself. While technically a member of the British Royal House, she had been taught by her Mama from her earliest years not to expect anything in the way of annual subsidies from the Privy Purse for she was: (a) too remotely related to matter; and (b) though technically the daughter of married, Royal parents, it was known to all and sundry that she was in fact a bye-blow of the late Buffy Strathmurder (later, and briefly, 16th Earl of that Ilk, before being shot dead by an irate husband). Brought up on her Mother's Kenyan farm, she had applied herself to farming and all things agricultural like a true descendant of George III. She was a fine, bouncing, tennis-playing young gel, the apple of Lady Mecklenburg's eye and the object of the attentions of numerous colonial swains.

However, the times – as the poet said – they were a-changin'. The Kikuyu were massacring and torturing their enemies in regular batches, establishing a reign of terror over many otherwise peaceful natives, and raiding and destroying remote upland farms. Somewhat late in life, Trixie decided to expand her horizons, and went off to study Chemistry at Pretoria University. Although her Mama thoroughly approved of this initiative, Trixie's departure left Lady Mecklenburg rather on her own at a time when she was becoming elderly, although she was perfectly safe, with a bodyguard squad of devoted ex-QORs. It was at this time that she obtained the services of her male nurse, Mr Blotts, a confirmed batchelor who had come out to the colonies many years before in the service of a retired Rear Admiral and who had remained ever since in similar service to a succession of doddery colonial toffs. He was, with his many years of experience, complete discretion and fund of catty stories and gossip about persons of quality, the ideal man for the job.

Trixie alas, found University life in the 'Sixties quite impossible for someone of her background and old-fashioned outlook. If she was going to continue there she would have to put up with either being regarded as a freak and therefore distinctly lonely, or conform. So, despite being a bit older than her fellow students, she invested in a few psychedelic mini-dresses, grew her hair down her back and all over her face, acquired several pairs of silly boots and started partying like there was no tomorrow. The effort, as the poet said, very nearly killed her. It did not stop her studying and passing her exams, nor did it bring about the downfall of the British Monarchy, but it meant she picked up some unfortunate habits, the worst being an addiction to certain harmful narcotic substances. By the time she graduated – with a Desmond of course, this being South Africa – she was well on the way to becoming a complete mess, and her life likewise. Her mother's disappearance in the Army helicopter caused a major breakdown, hospitalisation, and a long spell in the funny farm. The woman who emerged from all this after many months was by no means the Trixie Mecklenburg they had known and loved. She had become, in other words, a nut case and a heroin addict.

None of this was known about in Kibugoma. The Dergue assumed that their revered White Queen's daughter, having completed her studies at her far-distant seat of learning, would now return and take over her Mother's role on the sacred mountain of Kwakibu, according to the ancient ways of the Rugs. They wrote her an official letter to that effect which sent her spiralling into a renewed depression. "What the **** am I going to do?" she besought her shrinks, and her shrinks, as is the way with shrinks wheresoever in the world they may be found, gave a lot of conflicting advice in language only shrinks could properly understand, language usually referred to as Gobbledegook which, as anyone who has ever tried to decipher it well knows, makes learning Magongoese seem like sucking a lolly. Shrinks, let it be placed on record here if no where else in the universe, are useless bastards. But they make a good living at it.

So in other words, poor pooped-out Trixie was left to her own devices. On the one hand she could stay where she was in her sad, no-hope comfort zone along with her ministering shrinks and seedy chums, the scion of a Royal house become a junked-out nobody. Or she could start a new life far away, never lack for funds, say tatty-bye to the all-enveloping, pointless world of drug addiction, becoming White Queen of the Rugs, and probably go completely bananas in about three months. She tossed a coin. Unfortunately for the Rugs, it came down for the latter.

Great then were the rejoicings upon the sacred slopes of Mount Kwakibu when Queen Trixie first came among them. Drums went wild, dancers leapt and twisted, choirs sang their hearts out, feasting continued throughout that memorable day. Trixie, in dark glasses and an ill-fitting safari suit, her greying hair in a pony-tail, waved and smiled aimlessly. The Rugs were too intent on celebrating to notice anything odd. Only one guy noticed: Mr Blotts. He'd been wondering how he was going to occupy his time now that Princess Chrissie had flown away. Now he knew.

Trixie Mecklenburg

CHAPTER 30: LUDO.

Just how much more of this saga I would have learned from Grace Malumbwe I cannot say, for I never saw her again. She stopped coming. There was no explanation. Shortly after her last appearance, the cell guard came in with his usual tin dish one morning and announced: "You go wash and brush up, Mistah. Go see Mistah Ludo!" Then with another guy he half carried, half pushed me along the uneven passage to a room with a shower in it and a concrete floor with drainage. They put me in the shower and as the semi-hot water trickled down about me they got to work with scrubbing brushes and de-lousing powder. They cut off my long, filthy hair and gave me a quick shave. Glancing at my emaciated frame I noticed that I was no longer the muscular Adonis I'd once been – or fancied I'd been. They gave me a set of clean clothes – the old ones had rotted to the point of disintegration – and a pre-owned pair of Army boots. Clearly, Mr Ludo was not a man to suffer his refined sensitivities being affronted by the sight of a fellow human being looking and smelling like shit.

"How you feelin' now, fella?" asked my guard.

"Great," I said. "Really great."

"Good," he said. "You remember to tell Mistah Ludo how good we treat you here, Okay? You don't want to go bad-mouthin' us to the boss-man, do you? I mean, you probly be spendin' the rest of you life here."

"You can rely on me, Sarge," I said. "I've really enjoyed it here."

"Sure you have, fella," he said, smacking me on the head in familiar fashion. Then they pushed me out the door.

Two things troubled me when we finally got up the steps onto the ground floor: one was the bright daylight: it completely blinded me, and the other thing was my legs seemed to be too weak to keep me upright: I kept falling over. "My eyes!" I whined, holding my hands out before my face. "Dey all like dat when day come up from the cells" explained the Sarge. "Excep' the dead ones." But whether or not my fulsome praise for his tender loving care had softened his heart, he reached into a pocket of his shirt and took out a pair of cheapo sunglasses. "Here!" he said, thrusting them into my hands. "You give 'em back when you come down again." I put them on gratefully. "Cool, Man," he said. "They really go with the hair cut!"

The building, as it now appeared, was some sort of police post built by the Belgians from brick and roofed with corrugated iron. It had decent sized windows with metal gauze mosquito shutters and a high-walled courtyard outside. At its corners were watch towers. There was a heavy corrugated gateway for vehicles. A vaguely military boyo in sunglasses lounged against the shady side of the gateway, an automatic rifle cradled fondly in his arm.

Ludo was slumped in a battered wicker armchair, fiddling with a fly-whisk and occasionally killing passing buglife, an exercise he performed with unerring efficiency. His Army cap lay on his desk beside him, along with a few yellowing papers and an empty whisky bottle.

"Captain Voar!" he said. "Do come in, dear heart. You may go, Gentlemen." The guards left and, as they'd been holding me up, I fell over. "Goodness!" said Ludo. "You *have* been overdoing it!" He motioned towards a chair. "Think you can make it to that?" he asked. I crawled across the floor and jacked myself onto the chair. The exercise was just what I needed.

"So how are things, Captain?" he asked nonchalantly. "I understand you have no complaints about your living conditions. That's good. In fact, I've heard you've been managing to supplement your diet and even acquired a girl-friend. Quite the Scottish soldier, aren't we? Pity that Mrs Malumbwe recently met with an unfortunate accident. But then, these things happen. Don't they?" He paused: I stared at him. "Don't, they?" he repeated a little louder, smacking his leg with the fly-whisk.

"Why am I being detained here?" I asked.

"You are being detained here, m'dear fellow," he replied, "because I am kind. If I hadn't been kind you'd be rotting quietly in a pit along with the rest of your *kameraden*. I can still have you shot if that's what you'd prefer. Would you like that?"

"By what right am I being detained here?" I asked.

"By the right of every nation to its own self-defence," he said.

"You led an armed military reconnaissance unit deep into the territory of the DRC from a potentially hostile neighbouring state. You were soldiers but you wore no uniforms, which gives us the right to shoot you without trial as spies. Which is what we did. It is you that broke the law, Captain: that is why you are in jail: we have merely obeyed it."

"You are not the official agents of the DRC," I said. "You are not empowered to act for them."

"True," he replied, "and we are no longer living in an ideal world. The DRC as you well know, is a huge backward country, incapable of running itself like a well-ordered state. I and my gallant men happen to be looking after this part of it for want of a better alternative. We provide security, which the DRC central government cannot at present provide. Security from invaders like yourselves. The natives seem to find that acceptable."

"They have no alternative," I said.

"Quite," said Ludo. "That's the way it is. As I said, we aren't living in an ideal world."

"I have received no trial for my crime," I said. "How long is my sentence?"

"You are a prisoner of war," he said. "As such, and as is normal practice everywhere, you are detained till the war ends. That will not be tomorrow. I have told you before Captain: you are going nowhere. All traces of your ill-fated expedition have been removed from human gaze. The grave of your comrades is unmarked. Your three boats that you left at Ushwara have been chopped into little pieces, and Elder Ngwozo has burned the uniforms you left in his tender care. He will deny he ever saw you, because he does not want Jinjah shot up and torched. Then, back in Gwelo, there are people who remember sadly that you were decidedly overworked, stressed out, in need of a long rest, before you went off with a squad of men on some nutty expedition into the jungle. Plenty folk, they will say, go into jungles and never come back. They get eaten, contract fearsome diseases, are killed by criminal elements, go mad, or get swept away in the great grey green greasy Urumguano. Jungles are dangerous places to those not born there."

My heart sank. I had been written out of history.

"Your successor," added Ludo, "has been in post for almost a year."

I was, in other words, a dead man walking, or staggering. Alive, but without a life. Cheerful stuff to add to the depression. Even if I tried repeating the books of the Bible backward, I could only get to Habakkuk. I knew because I'd tried. Many times. Sitting in the cell chained to the wall. It was one of the things that was depressing me.

"Any further questions?" asked Ludo.

"What," I asked, "is Ponka?"

He levered himself out of the basket chair and opened a desk drawer, took out a packet a little longer than a Benson's pack and handed it to me. The front was emblazoned: Kibu Pharmaceuticals. Inside were three or four blister packs of tablets. On the back of the packet was a very long medical name for the product inside, and the message : "Anti-Depressants. Strictly for use as directed by Health Care Professionals."

"That's Ponka," said Ludo. "Try some."

"No thanks," I said and handed it back. He popped two and chucked them down his throat before tossing the packet back in the drawer. While he was on his feet he went to the door and shouted, "Corporal! Whisky! Chop Chop!"

"Ponka," he said, flopping back into the chair, "is why we're all here. Our *raison d'être* as it were. It's what's going on. And since you've come all this way, m'dear fellow, to find out what's going on, and since you won't ever be going away again, I reckon it would be churlish not to tell you the rest of it."

The Corporal came in with a bottle of "Mandingo's Magic Scottish Whiskey. Made in Gabon" plus a glass. He took the empty bottle away with him. "Best we can get hereabouts," said Ludo. "I expect you're an expert, being a Jocko."

"I know one when I see one," I said.

"As the actress said to the gay Bishop," he remarked, pouring himself a large glassful. "Pity the Corporal brought only the one glass. Tell me, should it be drunk neat or should one have some water in it? I have heard various opinions on that vexed subject. I do know that ice is an American abomination. But what about water?"

"About a centimetre of water to a double dram is about right," I said. "The stuff was never designed to be drunk neat."

"I am indebted to you, Captain," he said, rising. He opened the door and shouted for another glass. He was, as he had already said, kind.

"Ponka," he resumed after swallowing about half his glassful, "is the Rug word for the stuff with the long and unpronounceable medical name in that packet. Taken under strict medical supervision, it is apparently an effective, green substitute for Prozac and suchlike in the treatment of clinical depression. As such, depression being currently something of a worldwide epidemic, we have a worldwide market for it. Taken by the handful on the other hand, it is an extremely potent hallucinogenic narcotic stimulant which, among other various and exotic effects, can make one wildly energetic and aggressive for as long as you keep stuffing it down your gullet. Quite extraordinary. As such it is worth untold fortunes on the international drug scene, which is why, of course, Mistah Ludo and his chums have, following the collapse of some of our previous mercenary efforts, devoted ourselves to the marketing of it, no easy matter, ensuring its safe passage all the way from here then down the Urumguano to our despatching base in the docks at Cabinda, as corrupt an enclave as you'll see this side of the Gates of Pearl. A lot of palms have to be greased and quite a few greedy people shot. When it was just being developed, she tried out large batches on the Rugs and sent them rampaging all over the place, hyped up and convinced they were back in their tribal glory days when Rugs ruled the earth. They enjoyed themselves so much they came back every year and demanded repeat prescriptions. She went along with it, but gradually cut down the duration of the free handouts, as she went on refining the "Ponka.""

"Who's She?" I asked.

"She Who Must Be Obeyed, of course," said Ludo, refilling his glass. "The Great White Queen, Trixie Mecklenburg." Slurp. "Best bloody chemist north of Pretoria but mad as a hatter and far from healthy. Injects heroin two or three times a day. That's another of our responsibilities: to make sure she never runs out. When she came here first, her idea was to use her one asset, her knowledge of chemistry, in some way to help her people, the Rugs. There'd been various failed mining efforts which she re-examined but rejected. It had to be something that used raw material available locally. She noticed guys smoking Wuluwulu, and from then on she concentrated all her skill on making something highly marketable out of it, something that was light enough to shift over long distances without astronomic freight costs, something for which there was a lucrative market in rich countries. Her answer, after a long experimental process was Ponka. End of story. It's a brilliant answer and the profits are immense. Of course, she has a fair old wages bill: there's Ludoforce to be paid regularly for our marketing and security skills. There are several hundred Rugs up at Kibugoma: servants, staff of various kinds, a bodyguard – all of 'em with ceremonial robes or uniforms. Fortunately none of that is my responsibility. It's a huge place; a palace inside a fortress. God knows how old it is. It was restored by the Dergue during Princess Chrissie's time. And then there's the biggest responsibility of the lot of course: the Great White Queen Herself, who is physically and mentally a wreck and aging rapidly with it. I reckon she could go at any time. One man alone is in charge of all this: Mr Blotts, her nurse, sometimes referred to by us rude soldiery as the Small White Queen. He came here as a humble male nurse, and has extended his powers with spiderlike tenacity till not a ha'penny is spent but by his sanction, not a chair is dusted but by his order. Poor old Trixie is completely and hopelessly in his power, as he is in control of her supplies and the factory output. Somehow, all by his own cute little talents, he has established control to the extent that she can't make a decision without referring it to him. Occasionally he goes off for a few days fun and games at Zi Zi Mafudi's in Ushwara: God knows what he does there. When he's gone, Trixie goes completely bonkers, wanders around gibbering, asking over and over when Blotts is coming back. I'm not exactly a man who feels much pity, Captain, as you may well have noticed, but I feel sorry for the dear lady. I know mercenaries aren't paid to have feelings and I know it's all her own bloody fault and all that, but Blotts is a weird bastard, and he's fastened on her like a damned leech. In fact he's shaped her illness to his own advantage, if you ask me. She's more or less a bloody zombie because it suits him. For a soldier, Captain, well used to killing and all the bloody rest of it, there's something not quite nice about that."

He refilled his glass, and this time he refilled mine as well: the bottle was nearly empty. "Have another m'dear chap," he slurred. "Thing is, Captain, my Captain, and all that, you're going to need this bloody extra dram. Water? There you go. Don't think I'm pouring you another glass of Mr Mandingo's Magic Brew just out of the kindness of my heart. Oh dear me No. I'm pouring it because you're going to need a stiffener, old Son. Once I've told you what I am now about to tell you, you will feel the need of it. You may well be a bit wobbly. Yes, that's the word, the *mot juste*, as it were. Cheers!"

"God Bless!" I said. I gulped it down. Could there possibly be anything worse than I'd already had?

"Have another," he slurred.

CHAPTER 31: A WRASTLE WI' MISTAH BLOTTS.

"Thing is, er… Captain," Ludo continued after emptying his glass and refilling it with the remaining contents of the bottle. "Thing is…you're moving out of the cells."

I could hardly believe I'd heard correctly. "Hallebloodylujah!" I said.

"Don't celebrate too soon, chum," he said. "There are worse places than the Chiluba cells."

"Oh yeah?" I said. "Tell me about them."

"You're moving up to Kibugoma, at the personal request of Mr Blotts. The creepy bastard found out about you. Blighter knows everything that goes on, down to the minisculest detail. Bastard. Now he says he needs your services. Woops! Don't quite like the sound of that. Rather you than me, Matey, is all I can say. We can't really refuse him. It's true Mistah Ludo is the man to be feared in Chilubambashi, but Mistah Blotts is the power behind the throne, if you take my meaning. Everything depends on Ponka. Ponka depends on Trixie, and Trixie depends entirely on Mistah Blotts. Ergo, love him or loathe him, dear boy, Mistah Blotts is Number One Man, unprepossessing little sod though he undoubtedly is."

He got up, hauled the door open after some difficulty finding the handle and roared for another bottle. Clearly it really pained Ludo to be subservient to the dreaded Blotts. But I didn't give a monkey's. Blotts could be the Wicked Witch of the West for all I cared. The thought of getting out of that stinking, airless cell and moving to a palace in the good clear air of Mount Kwakibu filled me with joy.

"Have 'nuther, dear boy," slurred Ludo, only just managing to position the bottle accurately over my glass. "I don't mind if I do," I said.

The rest of that afternoon is a bit of a blur. I managed to get a shaving kit out of him and a badly-fitting tropical uniform. I even managed to change into it and pack the stuff they'd given me earlier into a plastic bag. At four o'clock or thereabouts an Army ten-tonner drew up in the courtyard and Ludo took me out and handed me over to the Corporal who was driving. It could have been Mandingo's Magic I suppose, or possibly the very thought of not having to return to the cells, but I found myself holding up pretty well on the short walk. I left the Sarge's sunglasses with

Ludo. "Take care, Captain," he said as the lorry moved off. "Don't say I didn't warn you."

The journey was rough, seldom out of low gears, the way no more than a rugged single-track. A smaller vehicle would have fallen to bits. It was hard to believe that along this rugged mountain track, batches of one of the world's most advanced pharmaceuticals were shipped out regularly, care of Mistah Ludo. Even more unbelievable was the vast brick fortress tucked into a precipitous valley near the top. I have never seen anything like it anywhere, although pictures of South American baroque cathedrals bear some resemblance except of course this place was devoid of Christian symbols. The brickwork alone at this level must have employed tens of thousands in the making, carrying and construction, then the whole thing had been stuccoed over to preserve the brickwork from erosion. Exuberant and highly inventive would be two words I'd use to describe it: the total opposite of the miserably mediocre junk they deem decent buildings in the Shetland archipelago. And there, standing in the huge arched entrance tower was a tubby little white man with his hands in his trousers pockets.

I marched up as smartly as I could manage to where he was standing. "Captain Voar reporting for duty, Sir!" I said, hoping thereby to create a favourable, no-nonsense impression.

He stared at me without showing the least indication he had heard. He had little piggy eyes, suspiciously black hair combed forward on his brow and a straggly moustache. His pudgy, yellowish flesh had plainly never been used to outdoor endeavour. At last, he spoke:

"Weel, weel. So du's Herbie Voar. Du'll no mind me, I doot. Few fok ever does."

Now it was my turn to stare in unbelief. Someone spikkin' Shetlan' hereaboots was about as likely as Jesus descending in a golden chariot from the sky. Slowly, as I gazed upon him, I got the feeling that somewhere long, long ago I'd seen this little tubby guy before.

"Du's...Du's..." I began.

"Soapy Blotts," he said. "Davy Blotts' boy fae Clugan. Davy o' Clugan dey aye ca'd him. I redder tink I wis i'da cless ahead o' dee at da aald Commercial. Does du no mind?"

Portions of my mis-spent youth flickered hectically before my mind's eye and, yes, there was a weedy fellow I could remember now, a total nonentity of a boy who got regularly pushed around, couldn't play football, was blate, never looked at the lasses, was poorly turned out and none too clean either. Soapy Blotts. The very last person in the universe you'd expect to find controlling a vast drugs empire and a Great White Queen in the heart of Africa.

"Foo's du doin' Soapy?" I ventured.

"Man," said he, "no sae ill, does du keen. Cam in trow."

He led the way into a vast barbaric entrance hall, its walls festooned with ancient weapons and tribal flags. Statuesque, uniformed servants stood stiffly at intervals along the muralled walls. From there we ascended a wide staircase and trudged along a very long corridor similarly lined with rigid attendants in coloured robes. Finally we came on a doorway with two servants outside it. At Soapy's nod they bowed and opened both leaves of the door for him to pass through without soiling his soft, pudgy hands. The doors closed silently behind us.

"Dis is a peerie bit different as wir aald twa-roomed croft hoose in Clugan," he remarked, sitting himself in a massive carved armchair. "Dip dee doon, Herbie. Dip dee doon, Boy. Du's oota da jail noo du keens."

I sat down on a comfortable chair for the first time in over two years. "Thanks," I said. "I spent my own early years in a shed up the old North Road, up behind Peter the butcher's. Me and about eleven or twelve others. We never did get aroond to countin' dem aal. So I can maybe appreciate whit du's sayin' aboot Clugan."

"Can du?" he said.

"I's very different nowadays," I said. "In Shetland I mean."

"Is it?" he said. "I'm never been back. Dad had TB eftir da War, and he deed in 1951. Eftir dat it wis juist her an' me. It's a mercy dae wir no more. We hed little i'da wey o' pennies, laek a lok o' idder fok danadays. Da hoose wis damp, wi' no piped water or electricity of coorse. We hed a few sheep an' a couple o' soor, ill-trickit rigs, an' dat wis dat. Shö wisna juist aesy to live wi. An dan eftir twartree years dey took her awa' to da hom. Eftir dat, hit wis juist me. I keend I wisna gret at onyting wi' me haunds, an' wisna muckle guid at da buik laere eddir, so I wis at a loss to keen juist hoo I wis to get a job. Dan Mither's sister, Sissie o' Twaxter, saw dis advert i'da pipper for a Male Nurse to attend some aald toff in Fetlar. Shö said if I applied, shö'd get me a suit o' claes to wear, so I did. I didna get the job, but I did get an interview, and eftir, da billie said he had a bridder sooth, an aald retired admiral boady, that needed some lookin eftir, an' if I wanted da job it wis mine. So dat's da wey hit wis. I hed neither trainin' nor experience but juist hed to pick it up. I surely must o' hed some sort o' knack, I suppose. Sissie let me keep da suit. Of course once you get sterted in dis line o' work there's aye plenty cast-aff claes – guid quality at dat – so I'm never hed to buy me a suit o' me ain yit.

"Da aald fellow, dey wir a bit of life in him yit, does du keen, an' I wisna six months there till he hed a notion to up sticks an' geeng ower to Kenya fur da sek o' da climate, and so I went along wi' him, an' never lacked for similar wark thereafter. Then of course da day cam whin som high boadies eskit me if I wid tak on Princess Chrissie. Weel, I'd always worked wi men boadies, but dis wis a bit o' an honour, shö bein' Royalty an' dat, so I juist tocht to mesel': Soapy me boy, dis hes got dy neem on it, so I took it. Minds du, Herbie, shö could be a proper whitrit o' a ting, Aald Chrissie, once shö sterted goin' doonhill. Will du hae a coarn o' tae ?"

"Anything, as long as it isn't porridge," I said. He pushed a little buzzer and about three minutes later two servants came in with trays: silver teapot, hot water jug, fine china, plates of delicate sandwiches, *petit fours*, an ornate ormulu cake-stand with an abundant selection of "fancies." Frankly, I doubt if even HRH the Prince of Wales – God bless and save him – does much better than that. "Man, Soapy," I said, "du's certainly come up in the world since Clugan."

"Yea," he said, "weel, maybe. But in Clugan I wis doin' eff all. Here I do hae a certain amoont o' responsibilities. Besides, aa dis pomp an' circumstance is juist to plase She Who Must Be Obeyed. If hit wis juist dee an' me haein' a scaur o' tae I su'd be sittin' by da Rayburn wi' me erse i'da restin' shair. Aald Chrissie insisted on royal etiquette throughoot da palace, and the Dergue at dat time backed her up. Her dat's noo here, shö's cam to be o' da sam opinion i'da end, though to begin wi', when shö fuirst cam, shö hed a slightly mair hippy style as it were. But gradually, we weaned her aff o' dat. Say whit du laeks, Herbie, there's no substitute for quality. I'm lived lang enyuch to keen dat, though I'm sure I dinna keen muckle o' ony value."

"You ought to write it all down, Man," I said. "It's a pretty unique story."

"Na, Boy, not I," he said, "I'd never mak much o' a writer. Can du read?"

"Read?" I said, surprised.

"Yea. Read oot alood, I mean," he said.

"Well, yes, I suppose so," I said. "It's not something I do often, but I reckon I can do."

"Guid," said Soapy. "Because dat's een of da twa reasons I'm gotten dee here. I'm no muckle öse at readin', du sees. I suppose i'da school I wis whit dey noo caas a dyslexic, though danadays dey preferred da term: Idle Peerie Bastard. Hit aa amoonts to da sam. I hae twartree Shetlan' stories I happened on when dey wir clearin' oot da brucks o' een o' me deceased patients. Dey wir i'da back of a draar. Gude keens hoo dey cam to be there, for he wisna a Shetlan' man an' I never heard him spik onyting idder as da King's English. But onywey, there dey wir. Dey'd been cut oot o' da Shetlan' Times awa back i'da 'Thirties when surely dey oesed to print twartree peerie Shetlan' stories in alang wi' da news an' stuff. Dey wir written by a fellow caa'd Joseph Gray. I dinna keen wha he wis, but to my unediccated mind, Herbie, dey really are most aafil gude, does du keen. Dey're aa aboot dis aald fellow caa'd Lowrie. Boy, he has some misanters! My favourite een is een caa'd "A Wrastle wi' a Hen." I could listen to him every day, I believe. I don't suppose noo, Herbie, if I gat him oot, does du tink du could maybe read him for me?"

"I'll certainly give it a try," I said. Compared to another night in

Chilubambashi jail this sounded like a doddle. So he went to a drawer in a hefty mahogany desk and took out a brown envelope with two or three yellowing, fragile newspaper cuttings in it, then I settled down to read him "A Wrastle wi a Hen." It was a story I came to know well.

CHAPTER 32: COME DAY, GO DAY.

I had reached journey's end. The long jail term had had a negative impact on my health, although I did make some recovery living in clean – if Spartan – quarters at Kibugoma. My days of jungle warfare and cross country yomping were over. At least that's what the depression told me.

I now had two duties to perform in exchange for my bed and board. One was to read Soapy his daily Lowrie story: the other was to do what I could to beef up the military skills of the Kibugoma Guard. It took most of the little energy I had, and I was usually glad when tea time came and I had to make my way to Soapy's royal drawingroom for Story Time. The guardsmen were fine chaps, but they certainly lacked for proper training and contact with other units. They were still armed with WW 2 rifles. Soapy had never been a military man but when I mentioned about the rifles he came to life. "Dir no need o' dat," he riposted. "We bought a quantity o' weapons when da Soviet Peace Mission went bankrupt in Upswapo. Du'll fin dem i'da guards' store."

When I checked, sure enough I found ten big crates full of new Kalshnikovs still in their grease and original wrappers. Just what a Peace Mission was doing with enough automatic rifles to take over power in a moderately sized African country was anyone's guess. "Does Ludo know about these?" I asked Soapy. "Whit's it got to do wi' him?" was his reply.

Soapy was, and remained throughout, an enigma. He was generally unapproachable and incommunicative, but then I suppose he always had been. A few short words was the most you'd normally get out of him, but at times without warning he would speak at considerable length, usually about incidents in his past life. Story Time was the only time I normally encountered him, so if I'd anything to say, that's when I said it. Sometimes, again without warning, he'd come out with morale boosting remarks such as: "Mind, Herbie, I can hae dee shot onytime I laek." or "There's no a livin' sowel i'dis place but I can snuff 'em oot laek a caunle." It seemed to amuse him, or reassure him maybe. Frankly, he needed to get out more.

Time went by. The Lowrie cuttings fell to bits: and I copied the stories carefully into a stout notebook. God forbid he should be deprived of his daily literary dose: then he might indeed start running around shooting everyone. There was "Lowrie Dines at Hillsook," "Lowrie Posts a Parcell at Lerook," "Up Against da Laa," and quite a few more. Eventually, I came to know most of them by heart, but Soapy never tired of them.

Soapy's Story Time.

Time, as I said, went by. His little piggy eyes missed nothing. One afternoon he suggested: "Why does du no try some o' dis Ponka for dy depression?" How did he know I was depressed? I wasn't wandering around weeping and threatening to shoot myself. I was wary of trying them, but of course, eventually I did. Taken strictly twice a day they did work and they were supposed not to be addictive, but who's going to give up something if it makes them a bit cheerier after a long period of gloom? So it went on. I settled into my daily routine, my comfort zone I suppose, and it was Come Day, Go Day. I couldn't have escaped even if I'd wanted to. The loss of my men had finished me. I still had all my marbles in normal working order, but I was living the life of a zombie. I was living, in other words, but had no life. I recalled what Ludo had said about Soapy and Trixie: "He's made her into a zombie because it suits him." and as I looked around me it dawned on me that this could be said of everyone who worked in Kibugoma. They all looked normal but all they ever did was passively follow instructions, routine. Their personalities were subdued though they were all competent at whatever their duties were, whether standing about as a servant or working in the Ponka factory. I was not the only one, I realised, going through this Come Day, Go Day routine: we were all in the same boat, a boat going absolutely nowhere except round in circles, at the will of the man with his hand on the tiller.

What about Trixie?

CHAPTER 33: THE GREAT WHITE QUEEN.

"So du wants to see HRH?" said Soapy. I studied his reaction carefully. It was the first time I had ever seen him look a bit shifty. "Dat can be arranged, my Jewel," he said. "She holds a public audience every Friday i'da big entrance hall. Aboot ten thirty."

I smartened myself up as best I could, got a hair cut, polished the boots. Would she be weird or royal? Maybe a bit like Princess Anne on speed?

The day dawned. A crowd flocked around the entrance. The numerous attendants were gorgeously arrayed. When we were all allowed in, all eyes focussed on the majestic, regal figure sitting on a throne several steps above floor level: a lady arrayed in white, erect on the throne, her arms on the armrests, a sceptre in one hand, a sword in the other: on her head a barbaric golden crown. She turned neither to left nor right.

A massive major-domo thudded the floor with his ceremonial staff, then commenced bellowing in Rug. Another guy struck a large gong. The first suppliant was summoned to approach the throne, which he did on all fours then rose and bowed low, such being the custom of the place. Some were there merely to present themselves – they had, many of them, come a very long way – others to present petitions which they read out aloud then handed to the Major-domo's clerk, sitting at a desk nearby. Then they joined the gathering in the hall until all the suppliants had presented themselves. Somewhere near the end of the procedings, the big man roared out: "Captain Herbert Voar, RMR!" and I crawled forward in the approved manner. If only because I was the only white guy among the day's petitioners, I'd half hoped HRH might perhaps have made some casual word of greeting, but it was not to be. Obviously, protocol is everything on such occasions, a protocol handed down perhaps from as far away as the Ancient Egyptians. Not to worry, I thought, no doubt when all this formal stuff is over, Miss Mecklenburg will descend from her throne on high and come for a brief walkabout amongst the lieges, asking them questions such as "What do you do, my good man?" or "Where are you from, churl?" just like the home life of our own dear Queen. At this point, however, a heavy curtain closed around the throne and servants appeared, wheeling trolleys with tea and sandwiches. The pipe band of the Queen's Own Rugs – preserved and maintained in fine

The Great White Queen.

form, complete with kilts – marched into the hall and struck up such favourites as Hey Johnnie Cope and Hieland Laddie, to the joy of the assembled lieges. They were followed by a team of acrobats and jugglers in the centre of the floor, whose antics and agility amazed everyone. Finally came native drummers and dancers whirling and leaping over the floor, to the claps and cheers of the crowd. Whether as a visitor attraction or as a cultural survival, the whole performance could hardly be equalled. But of the Great White Queen and her nurse there was, alas, no sign.

"Weel?" said Soapy at Story Time that afternoon, "whit did du tink?"

"As a piece of living history, great," I said. "But she's not exactly chummy, is she? I mean, your Royalty in this day and age generally press the flesh and exchange a few polite reflections with the great unwashed."

"Shö's as bliddy chummy as shö's ever going to be," replied Soapy. "Shö's been dead for six months."

I stared at him. This would indeed explain a certain stiffness in the performance. "So she's... She's been..." I hesitated.

"Stuffed," said Soapy. "No sae bad for an amateur, does du no tink?"

"You mean," I began, a bit lost for words and staring rather rudely at the tubby fellow, "you mean... you did the job yourself?"

"Dat did I, feth," he announced proudly. "Shetlan' folk aye hed to turn dir haunds til onyting, whin I wis a lad, du keens."

"Right," I said, edging my chair back a little. "Was she..."

"Dead?" asked Soapy. "Oh yes! Shö'd been ailin' for years and aye worsenin' du keens. Shö wis in a tarrable mess end up wi. Yea, shö wis dead aa right, nae fear o' dat. It wis a merciful release for her, but, minds du, it wis a bit o' a problem for da rest o' wis. But it wisna juist a big surprise. We'd seen hit comin', wi' da drugs an' dat. Da main ting wis makkin' sure da managers an' chemists at da factory wis aa properly genned up so dey could handle everyting demselves. Dat had lang been seen till. Shö'd lang been no muckle more as a casual spectator. And then, of course, I'd already given some tocht to how we wir going to arrange for da Great White Queen to continue. Dan I minded seein' i'da library, when we were clearing up eftir Aald Chrissie, dey wir a set o' hobbies books, simple, aesy-to-read books likely for ten-year-aalds or siclik, aboot stamp collecting, paintin' shaals, raffia work an dat."

He got up and extracted a slim volume from his desk drawer and handed it to me. It was called "The Gay Way Hobbies Series: Mummifying for Beginners."

"Hid's aal in there," he said, sitting down with the volume and leafing through it with apparent affection. "An simple enyoch, step by step, for a duffer laek me to juist aboot follow it. It cam in very handy I must say. Minds du, it wis a messy business to start aff wi', as du can maybe imagine, but, gi'e Trixie her due, by da time shö'd feenished wastin' her life, there wisna juist aal dat muckle fleesh a po' her? Thank Gude. Of course I had a couple of da boys helpin' me, but I hae to say, Herbie, I'm prood o' how we managed it: shö's cam oot weel, in my opeenion, and wi' luck, shö'll be sittin' up dere on yon tron for many generations to come, just laek yun aald Pharaoh boadies, du keens."

He was definitely chuffed that he had, probably for the first time in his life, mastered a fairly complex – not to say weird – manual skill. The trouble was, I feared, he was plainly thinking, like all hobbyists, of expanding his collection. "Does du keen, Herbie," he said, still leafing back and fore through the little book with its cute illustrations of the various stages of the mummifying process – gutting the body, preserving the flesh, stuffing, extracting the brain through the nose with a piece of wire – "I'm planning on tryin' a few more, juist so's I can get da knack o' da ting intil my brain. Dey wir nae money for hobbies whin I wis a boy, so – a bit late i'da day maybe – I'm takken ta dis laek a young lad wi' a new stamp album. It's a most absorbin' hobby. Dat aald Egyptians, du keens, dey wir at it day an' night. Even da bliddy cats wir done! Dey wid do a first class job on a Pharaoh or a Princess or som such, an' dan a mair sort of cheap-skate job for someen lower doon da peckin' order. Most intriguin,' does du no tink?"

"Er… yes," I replied, but I was starting to worry. Would I be next? Had Trixie really died a natural death or had Soapy found this book and got carried away, clapped his hands and got his two helpers to terminate what had become an increasingly difficult relationship? However, further reflection calmed my worries: I was irreplaceable as the sole reader of Lowrie stories. Others, however, it became apparent, weren't so lucky.

"Dat two guys," he continued, "dat helped wi' HRH. I'm workin' on dem noo. Weel, I tocht hit wis maybe da best wey o' keepin' dem quiet, but also of accordin' dem a measure o' immortality for their labours. Hit's takkin a bit langer, of course, haein' to do aal da wark mesel'. But da idee is, when they're feenished, I'll hae dem standin' fully robed on each side o' da tron, holdin' spears. Not a bad idee, Herbie? An' I wis winderan noo, if du could maybe gie me a peerie haund wi' dem. Du's a lok stronger as I am. Hit's really interestin' work, du keens. I'm sure du'll soon pick it up. Let's wis geeng doon there noo intil da cellars whaur I hae me bit laboratory, as I so caals hit. We could juist aboot get an hoor's work in afore supper time, if we got sterted right awa'."

I went with him, but only because, during the conversation I reached the conclusion, that Soapy was plainly nuts. He'd probably always been, but now it was coming to a head. He'd certainly been odd at school, and he'd had a poor home life as a child, gone out into the world entirely on his own at the age of fourteen to do a pretty awful sort of job for the rest of his working life. Then, since coming to Kibugoma with Princess Chrissie he'd taken on more and more lonely responsibilities, including a large and complex organization that would normally have employed several experienced managers. The guy was nuts and getting rapidly nuttier, and in the process I was going to have to take up a new hobby.

CHAPTER 34: HERBIE'S NEW HOBBY.

I am not going to narrate in detail how we mummified those two Rugs, and I feel sure any normal persons reading this will be glad of that. Those with any interest in such matters could always obtain a copy of the Gay Way book and study it for themselves in some quiet, secluded spot. The Shetland Times bookshop in Lerwick is first rate at obtaining obscure volumes for its customers, though as this one was published in the 'Thirties it might prove elusive. And if still in print, the series might possibly have changed its name.

Besides taking up mummifying, I now gave up Ponka. It wasn't easy, but I reckoned I was going to need all my wits about me from now on to cope with Soapy. I also began, to fight my depression instead of just learning how to cope with it. It was truly like a devil fastened on your back. Winston Churchill – no coward and no weakling – called it his "black dog." And he certainly managed to make his mark despite it. I began to think how totally pointless it was to go over and over about the massacre of my men on the road to Chilubambashi. Ludo had never pretended to be anything other than a hired killer. That was his job: to secure the Kibugoma Rug enclave by any means, plus its lucrative trade. He was no more a monster than any other active soldier. He had set a trap for us, due to receiving information about our movements: he could as easily have got the information from the lorry driver as from Madame Mafudi. Whatever way it was, he'd won that round and we'd lost. So what? That's what life is all about. Churchill didn't go off into the sulks for the rest of his life because the Gallipoli campaign was a calamitous failure. Neither did Hitler spend his years quietly weeping because he got tossed into the nick at an early stage in his illustrious career. By re-thinking along such lines, and by giving my brain a regular kicking to boot out the self-pity, I began to make some headway. My old self was in there somewhere, deep down under layers of woe, and I reckoned he could be kicked back up to life. Mummification had not yet occurred, and I had to make bloody sure it didn't.

No longer having any nursing duties to occupy his time, Soapy now had more time to spend on his new hobby. How long, I wondered, before half the population of Kibugoma was away with the Pharaohs? It meant that he and I were in each other's company a lot more, down there in the mummifying lab. Perhaps because I was a fellow Shetlander, he became a bit more chatty than had been his wont, telling me tales fron his macabre life as an old toff's nurse, and going on to discuss the complex affairs of Kibugoma that he had to rule over as substitute for the Great White Queen. The role of the Dergue remained shadowy: how far were they involved in the lucrative marketing of Ponka? When he talked about such matters, Soapy became apparently normal: it was like chatting to one's bank manager (in the days when there were normal bank managers). Yet we were chatting in a secret mummifying lab.

Another change now that HRH had gone to be with Anubis and Amon-Ra, was that Soapy could get off a bit more often for a trip down to Ushwara, to check into Madame Mafudi's health farm, without incurring the tantrums of Trixie on his return. In his absences, I made a thorough exploration of as many of his rooms as I could gain entrance to because the servants on the doors knew me well. It was his first floor audience chamber where we foregathered every afternoon for Story Time that attracted my closest attention, because somewhere in there was a safe. And guys who earn a living marketing highly desirable drugs worldwide do not get paid in used Bank of Scotland fivers. They get paid in gold bars.

Usually, he was away three days, saying nothing to anyone about it either before or after. Then came a time he was gone five days and I'd been thinking he was surely getting his money's worth, when a servant came and told me to go to the phone. It was Ludo.

"It's your Boss-man," he said without preliminaries. "He's snuffed it. At Madame Mafudi's."

"Died on the job did he?" I queried.

"Er, not exactly," said Ludo. "What am I to do with him?"

"Bring him here and take him round the back. We don't want people to know about it right away. There will be problems. Round the back. I'll be waiting for you."

From the back entrance we took Soapy down into his own lab, and I put him in the fridge. He could stay there indefinitely.

"I've never been in here before," said Ludo casting a casual glance over the premises.

"It's a recent addition," I explained. "What exactly happened?"

"According to Zi-Zi," said Ludo, "he wanted to buy a girl – which is perfectly legal and happens every day somewhere in these parts – but he then wanted to give her a lethal injection, then bring her back here. Something about a handmaiden for the Great White Queen. Weird bastard."

"That makes sense," I said. "Then what happened?"

"One of Zi-Zi's bouncers came in and clubbed him. He went out like a light. That's all."

I looked at Ludo. "I have a proposition for you," I said, "but first, I just want to tell you I reckon what you did to my men falls within the rules of war. Only just, but definitely. Just thought I'd let you know that."

"Okay," said Ludo. "What's the proposition?"

A week later in the middle of the night, I left Kibugoma with all my meagre luggage in the back of one of Ludo's ten tonners. Half the contents of Soapy's safe came with me: the other half stayed with Ludo. It was a long and uncomfortable trip, but it was free from any kind of interference, either bureaucratic or criminal or military. Fifty of Ludo's finest thugs ensured total security in armoured vehicles before and aft. Nobody wanted to get in our way. Three days later, I was in Kinshasa.

I felt very strange standing in a bustling city street: strange and dizzyingly free! One of Ludo's cars took my ingots to the Herzog von Anhalt private Swiss bank: they were used to rough, unshaven types off-loading gold bars there. The other car took my few goods and chattels to the airport. I said Goodbye to Sgt Boma, whom Ludo had put in charge of the operation, but found that Ludo had instructed him not to leave town till they'd seen me off on the plane. So two beefy men in dark glasses and bulky jackets accompanied me for the rest of the day. "Plenty bad mans in 'Shasa,"

Shopping in 'Shasa.

said the Sergeant. I bought a few things I was short of: shoes, a suit, clean clothes, a wallet, a submachine gun – the usual stuff people need when they get out of jail. "Feel better now?" asked Sgt Boma.

I'd already left Magongo far behind, and at 6a.m. next morning, as the Congo Airlines Tupolev 111 climbed steeply into the tropic sky, I finally left Africa. That night I was in London, feeling very cold and having to buy a jersey and a thick jacket at their exorbitant airport shops, and by the following afternoon – quite unbelievable really – I was lying around Aberdeen airport waiting to find out if the Sumburgh plane was going to take off or not, due to fog. Some things never change. It was even colder here. Weirdest of all, I glanced at my ticket and found the date was 2008! 2008!!! Blimey! I somehow thought we were still in the nineteen nineties! When I got home, I'd be able to apply for my Old Age Pension!

CHAPTER 35: IN THE VALLEY OF THE PHARAOHS.

Well, of course, it was now I found out how foresighted I'd been all those years ago when I'd got Cooncillor Ertie Spence to get me No. 4 Provost Freebie Drive, Lerwick. Not only did I find my collection of aald bikes still intact in the front room, but here I had a home of my own without further fuss or expense. Maybe some of you will be saying: A guy with a big stash of gold bars in a Swiss bank could surely get himself a bit better hom as that, but that's not the way I saw it. I would have felt entirely out of place anywhere else, and I think after all my recent experiences I was due a few home comforts.

Then there was Soapy to consider. I mean, how oot-o'-pliss would he have felt in a plush new bungalow in Gulberwick? Na, na, Boys. Provost Freebie Drive was da very pliss for him to spend his declining years.

They delivered him next day, and though I say it myself, I really do think I'd made a most particular job of him, especially as the whole job had to be done at record speed. As luck would have it, I had an aald restin' shair I'd got fae wir Chimmie at Mid Yell after Aald Daa passed away. I had it in the kitchen alongside the Rayhurn an' dat's juist whaar we plonkit doon Mistah Blotts. Tell you the truth, I'd had something of the sort in mind when I mummifed him, so I'd made him in a sitting doon position and he fitted brawly weel intil da aald restin' shair. He had ee hand on his knee, and i'da idder I geed him a cup and sasser, wi' twartree peerie fancies a'til it. It was pretty lifelike. His peerie mooth wis open as if he's tellin' wis da laetest news. Later, once I got organised, I had him wired for soond, and eftir dat, weel, in ahint da lapels o' his jacket I had a set o' controls putten' in. Then aal du had to do is press the appropriate button, and Soapy'll stert up wi' "A Wrastle wi' a Hen" or "Lowrie Dines at Hillsook" or whatever een taks dy fancy. There's a few folk come in and seen it: quite a few in fact. An' sometimes, eftir twartree drams, an' we're aal sittin' yarning it's aesy to forget he's juist a poor stuffed fellow, and soon du tinks he's takkin' pert i'da conversation an' ferly enjoyin' himsel'. Gude keens, he didna hae muckle enjoyment in this world, so he's better aff noo in mony weys as he ever wis.

Of course, there had to be adjustments when Nort Isles Nora cam to share wir life, what wi' da front room full o' motor bikes an' da kitchen haein' peerie Soapy sittin' aboot aal day wi' his sasser o' fancies. "A'm no haein' yun daed bugger sittin' aboot in my bliddy kitchen aal day!" she said. I suppose she had a point, and after all, Soapy wis never onyting to her. So efter a bit o' argie-bargie, we moved Soapy intil da front room, and I got een o' dis big crofter's sheds ootside i'da gairden for da bikes. Matrimonial peace was restored, and, does du keen, I believe Soapy is better plased in there. I mean, he wis aye ösed to mixin' wi' dis high boadies maist o' his adult life, so da kitchen wis maybe a bit doon-merkit for him. Also, when wir Nora cam to stay, shö said she'd want something a bit mair moadren i'da wey o' furnishins as da aald three piece suite in uncut moquette that had been i'da front room since aboot 1972, though mind you it wisna juist in bad shape for aa. Shö replaced it wi' some of dis trendy leather swivelling armchairs. So I pit Soapy intil een o' dem, an' noo he can birl him aboot as weel as juist sit there, an' look oot da window at da passin' scene.

Soapy sits it oot.

Weel, I'm had me say, I suppose. There's laekly no mony Shetland folk interested in aa dis spiel aboot Africa an' dat, far less in da mysteries of mummification. But I'm prood of me bit o' wark nevertheless: It wisna aesy, especially i'da circumstances o' da time. Soapy wis right. It is an absorbin' hobby, and now I'm gotten me act together once again, I think we're now in a position to offer the Shetland public a service it has lang been needing.

It just seems to me, and to my two born-again nephews, Ulf and Grit who've joined me in this venture, that today's affluent Shetlander has come to be a man who has it aal. He has the latest four-be-four, the biggest possible modern hoose, a fine big yacht, the most exotic holidays on far-distant strands, and his wife is aye dolled up to the nines and sittin' aroond in her sun lounge wonderin' whit else they can get.

As a business man, I think I have the answer. Yes: Mummification. Whit's da use of accumulatin' aal dis proil, if, within a few days o' braethin' dy last, du's either stuck inunder da ert an' instantly forgotten, or else brunt til a peerie box o' cinders? Today's affluent Shetlender deserves and can surely do a lot better as that! I mean, dis aald funerals wis maybe aal right i'da aald days when dey had little money. But times has changed, an' we're no needin' noo juist to creep awa' inunder da ert laek a bliddy slater. That's why we at Voar's VALLEY OF THE PHARAOHS say:

Yes We Can! We can guarantee you an Eternity befitting your wallet! We can give you the sort of send-off you've worked hard for all your life! And we can offer a variety of styles to suit all pocket! *FIRST*, there's our ECONOMY DO IT YOURSELF MUMMIFICATION PACK, where we do the gutting, then your grieving relatives get a full set of instructions, three economy size packs of eco-friendly stuffing, plus needles and thread to complete the job in their very own style, so's you can sit around forever after at home, still part of all those precious moments of family togetherness.

SECOND, there's our QUEEN OF THE NILE FULL MUMMIFICATION DEAL, where we do the lot, rig you out in full Pharaoh kit – wig, crown, false beard, black eye liner and simulated marble throne – plus free plot for a hundred years in our recently built Temple of Amun-Ra out at our Valley of the Pharaohs premises at Clugan, next to our Soapy Blotts Memorial Laboratories. *THIRD* and last, for the seriously rich modern trendy Shetlander who has truly managed to cram everything into his life on Earth, we respectfully suggest our EVERLASTING GOLD OF THE PHARAOHS TREATMENT: full, first-class mummification with Gold, Frankincense and Myrrh, plus hand-carved, gilded sarcophagus, funeral procession featuring High Priests of Ra, Eunuchs and Slave Girls playing nose flutes and harps, plus final entombment in YOUR VERY OWN PYRAMID at the top end of our VALLEY OF THE PHARAOHS! What a way to go! Talk about Go out with Style! (And by the way, two mummified slave girls can be supplied at extra cost to accompany you to the Land of the Dead, but these have to be ordered in advance from the Democratic Republic of Congo).

So that's it then. I hope you've enjoyed me memoirs, and, better still, I look forward to making your closer acquaintance when you opt for one of our three great bargain offers (above). (Special terms available for S.I.C. Cooncillors). Always remember what Karl Marx said:

> When you have grabbed your last ten quid
> And downed that final glass,
> They're playing "I Did it My Way"
> and they're phoning for the hearse,
> Remember! You don't have to go,
> You can stick around some more,
> And last into Eternity,
> If du's signed up wi' Herbie Voar!
> At our Valley of the Pharaohs,
> We'll preserve you for all time,
> Lookin' good and just as handsome
> As you were in your prime.
> Just like Tutenkhamun,
> You'll live for evermore:
> Proof that you CAN take it with you
> – If du's signed up wi' Herbie Voar!
> (Yes we Can!)